LIVING IN
SHADOWS

02 16

Living in Shadows
by Jessica Freeburg
Published by Clean Reads
www.cleanreads.com

For Landon, Logan, Ella, and Brielle.

CHAPTER ONE

VIVIAN SAT SILENTLY IN THE PASSENGER seat of her father's black Mercedes. Under different circumstances, she would have enjoyed riding in such a nice car. But now, she would give anything to sit in her mother's weather-beaten, wood-paneled station wagon one more time.

She could easily imagine the rattle the engine made, whenever her mother accelerated. "Over 200,000 miles and still going strong!" her mother bragged, the only one who could have been proud of such a dilapidated box of bolts and oil.

"I think it's falling apart from the inside out," Vivian always said.

Her mother patted the steering wheel. "She's a little shabby, but she's still got some life left in her!"

"When can we get an Escalade?" Vivian asked, half-joking. She knew an Escalade was not in their future. Though her mother struggled to make ends meet, she always made sure Vivian and her younger brother, Thane, had everything they needed. That didn't always equate to having everything they wanted, but they had enough.

Vivian jostled in her seat as the sedan dipped through a large pothole, the jolt pulling her back into reality. She could feel the chill of the tan leather even through her jeans, making her shiver.

"These roads need some work," her father mumbled. She didn't bother responding. Vivian hadn't spoken since he'd picked her up at the airport two hours ago, and she had no intention of breaking her silence now. Why would she? Before the accident, he hadn't bothered to call for almost a year. Ten months, one week, and two days—not that she was counting.

Their relationship had been strained, following her parents' divorce. Visits were sporadic. A weekend one month, but not the next. Maybe a visit over Christmas break, maybe not.

At first, Vivian and Thane had begged to see their dad. But he canceled more plans than he kept, leaving them both heartbroken, and over time, angry. Eventually, they realized the only thing they could count on, when it came to their father, was that they *couldn't* count on him at all.

Vivian and Thane always hoped that one day he would magically return to the dad they had known before the divorce. The dad who was home every night to tuck them in with a kiss. The dad who took them to Yankees games and gave them piggy-back rides to the park. The dad who taught Vivian to ride her bike without training wheels. Mom had taught Thane. By the time Thane was big enough, *that* dad was already gone.

"This is the longest ride ever! Has your butt fallen asleep yet?" Thane whispered from the back seat.

Vivian kept silent and tried not to smile. She watched the blur of trees darting past her window. In the dim moonlight, Vivian could see their branches, dressed in red, yellow, and orange leaves, extended toward the sky, as if they'd just been busted by the cops. Moonlight peeked from behind a gray cloud, casting jagged shadows across the road ahead of them.

Vivian had never seen so many trees. She was more accustomed to skyscrapers and concrete than the twisted, skeletal branches that clawed toward her as she peered through tinted glass.

Her father drove on, unspeaking, until they bounced through another pothole.

"This road is ridiculous." He forced a smile as he glanced at Vivian. Deep dimples that matched her own dented his cheeks. Thin lines frowned from the corners of his blue eyes. Vivian couldn't help but notice the dark circles that puffed beneath them. He looked so tired that she almost felt sorry for him. He must have hated the thought of being saddled with a sixteen-year-old as much as she detested being stuck with him. "I'm sorry. There are so many stupid pot holes, I can't avoid them all!"

"No problem," Thane retorted. "At least all this bouncing around is keeping my butt cheeks from falling asleep! Did that last bump wake yours up, Viv?"

Although she was happy to have him along, Vivian tried to ignore her brother. If she smiled, her father might think she was smiling at *him*, and she didn't want there to be any confusion about how much she loathed him, and the idea of moving in with him and his new wife.

Turning off the highway, the sedan weaved onto a narrow road and began snaking between rows of weeping willows. Their sagging branches hunched over as if they were too depressed to stand up straight.

Vivian grasped the armrest that ran along the side of her door, digging her nails into the tan leather. The road was so narrow that she wondered what they'd do if they met an oncoming vehicle. They'd need to drive into the grass to avoid a crash.

Vivian eyed the thin strip of ground between the road and the evenly spaced tree trunks. She quickly surmised the space was much too small for a vehicle. Her heart beat at her chest as her father sped across the pavement. She wished he'd slow down.

If they met an oncoming car, they'd either barrel into it head-on or swerve into a tree. She wondered what type of damage a tree would do to her father's Mercedes. She already knew how the collision of metal against metal could mangle and destroy.

Vivian's body became rigid as she squeezed her eyes shut, willing herself to somehow lock out the memories with her eyelids. She struggled desperately to rebury the images of a moment too awful to recall, but so fresh, they boiled on the surface of her every thought.

She could hardly comprehend how one day could turn her life inside out like a worn shirt, tossed on the floor. If only she hadn't forgotten her Algebra assignment on the table. If she'd put it in her backpack the night before, they wouldn't have been returning home on the southbound freeway. They would have been safely at school by the time that man got on the freeway. In one shattered moment, her life became clouded with guilt.

She tried not to blame herself for the accident. Everyone said they were simply in the wrong place at the wrong time, and the only one to blame was the drunk who had entered the freeway heading in the wrong direction. Of course, that's what people are supposed to say to survivors of tragedies, even if it *was* their fault. No one's going to say, "Hey, kid, nice job making yourself an orphan!"

Vivian had been bewildered by the idea that anyone could drink so much the night before, they would still be intoxicated at seven forty-eight the next morning.

Seven forty-eight.

Thane had announced the time just seconds before the collision. He had been so upset that they were going to be tardy, thanks to Vivian's carelessness. In a fraction of a second, being tardy didn't matter anymore. Nothing mattered

4

anymore.

She rubbed her hand unconsciously across her forehead, her fingers tracing the thick skin that had been stitched shut above her eye.

"It wasn't your fault," Thane whispered.

Turning in her seat, she looked at her brother's round, dimpled cheeks as he smiled reassuringly at her. His blue eyes sparkled as moonlight bounced off them in the darkness of the backseat. Vivian wiped at a tear as she took in his features. A splash of light freckles danced across the bridge of his turned-up nose and tanned cheeks. Sandy blond hair touched the tops of his eyebrows. His baby face camouflaged his fourteen years.

Thane seemed to read her mind most of the time. She wondered how he could do that. Most of *them* could.

"I'm still here." His voice floated into Vivian's mind like the white puff of a dandelion blown in the wind.

"It's not the same," she responded without speaking.

"What is it, Vivian?" her father asked, interrupting her thoughts. Furrowing his eyebrows, he squinted at her while she stared sadly into the empty backseat.

"Nothing," she mumbled, angry she had to break her silence. She turned her body around to look out the passenger window, hoping he wouldn't ask any more questions. What could she say? *Don't mind me, Daddy. I'm just talking to your dead son, Thane. Didn't Mom ever mention I talk to ghosts?*

"You should say that! He'll think you're nuttier than a squirrel's turd!" Thane laughed from the backseat.

"You sound like Mom. That's something she would have said." Vivian couldn't help smiling at the thought of her mother's propensity to speak like an 80-year-old-redneck from somewhere in the deep South. She'd referred to this type of witticism as "proverbs", but Vivian wasn't sure most of her mother's crude one-liners should share the name of any book in the Bible.

She set her jaw and let go of the happy feeling, before her

father could notice the slight grin reflecting off the blackened window she stared through. Vivian focused her thoughts instead on the sorrowful trees that blurred past, as her father sped over the bumpy blacktop.

His speed decreased, and the rows of willows that hugged the narrow boulevard reflected in her rearview mirror. A variety of deciduous trees dotted a flat patch of freshly trimmed grass ahead of them, their tops a burst of red and orange against the pale, white light of a full moon.

Vivian's eyes traveled from one tree to the next, as she stared across a yard larger than any football field she'd ever seen. It took her a moment to realize the long path they'd been traveling on was actually the driveway leading to her new home.

The paved lane concluded in a circle at the bottom of several rows of steps ascending to an immense, brick structure, which was skirted by a porch that disappeared around the corners of each side. Vivian's gaze settled on the double-doors, painted a deep crimson, centered at the top of the steps. In the dim porch light, the doors looked like an opened mouth.

As her father parked at the base of the steps, Vivian instinctively pulled her body away from the house looming in front of her. The sharply arched windows of the imposing three-story structure glistened in the moonlight, reflecting the twisted, bare trees surrounded it.

"Home sweet home," her father said with fake enthusiasm. Vivian peered through her window at fallen leaves fluttering across the porch, which was framed by brick and thick, white pillars.

What a cheese head, she thought, waiting for her brother to agree. When she gazed into the backseat, it was as empty to her eyes as it was to her father's. *I guess I'm on my own,* she thought miserably.

Before Vivian could protest, her father opened her door.

Regarding her with weary eyes, he smiled, offered his hand and asked, "Can I help you out?"

"No thanks," Vivian looked past him as half of the house's door-mouth burst open.

A pretty, petite woman bounced down the steps, her blonde hair bobbing with each footfall.

"Hello, Vivian! I'm Rebecca," she smiled sweetly. Her voice carried softly on a gust of wind that shook the tree branches in the yard, raining dried leaves over the trio. Rubbing her bare arms gently with her hands, Rebecca shivered, peered across the lawn at the scattering dead leaves, and exclaimed, "It's chilly! Let's get you inside."

Reaching into the car, the woman took Vivian's hand before she could object. "James, grab her bags. I've got hot chocolate waiting for us." Rebecca wrapped one arm around her stepdaughter's shoulder, still firmly grasping Vivian's hand.

Although Vivian wasn't sure she wanted such a greeting from this woman she presumed to be her stepmother, it felt good to have someone shielding her from the cold. It felt warm and comforting. It felt motherly.

She let herself melt into the warmth of her stepmother's arms. Closing her eyes, she imagined her own mother holding her. But a familiar ache tore at Vivian's heart, the moment she opened her eyes and found herself being led across the porch toward the open door. She crossed the threshold and was swallowed into the house—ripped from the world she knew and sucked into a strange life she wanted nothing to do with.

She hadn't realized she'd been holding her breath, until it puffed loudly through her lips as she scanned the entryway of her new home. The air was thick as she inhaled deeply. On the surface, the smells were pleasant, but somewhere beneath the scent of burning wood mingled with freshly baked cookies, there was something else. A metallic and unpleasantly familiar odor that made Vivian's knees lock and her legs unable to move forward.

Her head became light, and the grand staircase with a carved mahogany banister began to sway in front of her. Vivian tightened her grip on her stepmother's hand as her legs buckled. The tiny woman held her up, nearly carrying her across the marble floored foyer into a dimly lit room.

The room faded to black as Rebecca gently eased Vivian's limp body onto a chenille sofa. For a moment she was paralyzed. Her mind screamed at her body to move, while the nauseating, metallic smell overpowered any other scent. A fire crackled nearby, but seemed to give off no warmth at all. She was conscious of nothing but an intense, unearthly chill and *that* smell.

A deep, unending darkness overpowered the light around her.

CHAPTER TWO

BLACKNESS SWALLOWED HER AS HER FATHER'S voice swam through the murkiness.

"What happened?"

Vivian wondered the same thing. She willed her eyes to open, only to find them stuck shut.

"Oh, James! I think it's all a bit much for her. I'm sure she's just overwhelmed. Get me that pillow, please."

That must be it, Vivian thought. *I just passed out because I'm exhausted!* But what was that awful smell? Why did it seem so familiar? Vivian's mind raced through memories as she tried to place it. *How can it feel colder in the house than it had felt outside?*

Hands raised Vivian's head, as a pillow slid below the base of her neck. Her hair was smoothed away from her face, as she sluggishly opened her eyes. The dim light from the fire made her eyes snap shut.

"See, she's coming around. Vivian, honey, are you alright?"

Slowly, her eyes opened. Her stepmother knelt beside her, clearly concerned.

The strange smell was gone. The chill that made her unbearably cold only moments before was replaced with the warmth she had expected to feel upon entering the house. It had to be the stress of coming here, or the fact that she hadn't slept much in the days before the move. She reasoned she was simply so tired and overwhelmed that her mind was playing tricks on her.

"I'm sorry," Vivian stammered. "I don't know what happened. I just got dizzy." As she sat up, the room began to spin again. Red curtains blurred into mahogany paneled walls, as the flames within the white marble fireplace quivered erratically. She let her head fall lightly back onto the pillows.

She hated feeling helpless. She wanted to sit up, walk stubbornly to her bedroom, wherever that was, close the door behind her and not come out until tomorrow or maybe the next day. She could probably survive at least a couple days on the bag of peanuts she stashed in her pocket on the airplane. But her body wouldn't move—it refused to cooperate.

"Don't apologize. You've been through a lot. Just take some deep breaths and try to relax." Her father's hands still smoothed her hair gently. "Rebecca, let's prop another pillow behind her back so she can sit up a little more."

She looked up at him wanting to scream, *Don't try to play Daddy now!* Instead she heard herself simply say, "Okay."

Her stepmother gently positioned another pillow as Vivian closed her eyes and took deep, cleansing breaths, the kind her mother took when she'd practiced yoga in their living room. Vivian had only been away from the cramped, two bedroom apartment she'd shared with her mother and brother for two weeks, but it already seemed like a lifetime ago that she'd packed up her things and gone to stay with her mother's friend, while the final arrangements were made for her trip here.

Here—in the middle of nowhere. Where the only sounds she'd heard so far were the first of Fall's leaves being shaken from their branches in the cool October breeze. No traffic buzzing outside the window, or horns honking. No voices shouting. Not even the hoot of an owl.

Here—where a pretty, young stepmother wanted to dote on her, and her father wanted to pretend to care, after he'd spent so many years not giving a crap.

Taking another series of deep breaths, she opened her eyes.

"Would you like something to drink, Vivian? I've made hot chocolate. Or I could get you some water," Rebecca's voice held a tone of genuine concern.

Her smile was gentle, not fake or overdone. Other than clear gloss glistening on her naturally pink lips and a coat of mascara that darkened her long lashes, her skin was free of makeup. Her light blonde hair, cut just below her chin, revealed a gracefully thin neck. Vivian could see why her father had married her. She possessed a kind of natural beauty, that made women jealous and men swoon.

"No thank you," Vivian mumbled. "I'd just like to go to bed."

"We've got a room ready for you upstairs," Rebecca replied as she steadied Vivian with one hand and helped her to her feet with the other.

"I'm okay," Vivian mumbled as she nervously pulled her long, golden-brown hair over her right shoulder, twisting the ends around her fingers. "Thank you."

She managed to be courteous, but avoided eye contact. She was afraid if she looked into anyone's eyes, she might burst into tears and fall back onto the soft cushions of the sofa again, blubbering about how miserable she was. She followed her stepmother into the foyer, focusing on the shades of gold and cream swirled randomly through the marble floor beneath her feet.

Her legs felt like concrete as she plodded up the steps behind Rebecca. Her father followed, carrying two bags—a large, pink suitcase that had been her mother's, and a black duffle bag that had belonged to Thane. Those two bags contained everything she managed to salvage from her old life. She swallowed hard, trying to hold back the bile that rose in her throat, as she was led like a prisoner to her cell.

"I thought you might like this room." Rebecca motioned toward the open door just around the left corner of the top step. "I found a few things from the attic I thought you'd like, but you can change it however you want to make it your own."

The wide staircase concluded at a broad landing, which was open to the foyer below. A lavish chandelier hovered above, twists of gold and crystal shimmering in the glow of its pale light. Vivian's mind swam in a cloud of exhaustion. She was barely aware of anything beyond the polished wood creaking beneath her feet as she climbed upward.

Each stride brought her closer to her room. She could hardly wait to shut the door and bury her face in an unfamiliar-smelling pillow, and cry until her chest ached. She just wanted to be alone. But with each step, the hairs on the back of her neck began to rise and gooseflesh broke out on her arms. There must have been a window open somewhere.

Maybe they're airing out the bedroom, she reasoned.

A light gust of air blew stray strands of hair away from her face, almost as if an unseen being had rushed past her. Vivian shivered against the chill.

"Don't go in there!" Thane whispered urgently.

Vivian had to grab the banister to keep from falling backward. The sudden sound of Thane's voice almost made her jump.

"Why not?" she asked Thane silently.

"There's a shadow spirit in there. It's a bad one. I saw a room on the other side of the stairs. It's closer to Dad's room at the end of the hall. Just tell them you'd rather have that one." Thane stood at the top of the stairs peering nervously toward the room

Rebecca had pointed to.

Vivian's feet planted on the second step from the landing, causing her father to stop abruptly to avoid crashing into her back.

Rebecca was still walking toward the room. "I've always thought this pink room would be perfect for a girl."

"*Stay away from the door, Vivian. This shadow is evil. You can't let it know you can see it!*" Thane disappeared before the dark spirit could see him speaking to Vivian.

"Where's your bedroom?" Vivian pretended not to know as she turned toward her father.

"It's just at the end of the hallway," he replied pointing away from the room where Rebecca was standing in the open doorway. She'd already flipped the light on. Pale pink wallpaper dotted with tiny white and fuchsia flowers burst into view behind her.

A shadowy figure darted across the dimly lit room like a large, black dog rushing to examine an unfamiliar house guest, pausing just inches from Rebecca. It was at least a foot taller than her, even as it stood in front of her hunched over awkwardly, partially hidden from Vivian's view by the bedroom wall flanking the doorway in which her stepmother stood. Its head cocked sharply to one side as it seethed like an angry cat.

Vivian wanted to scream for Rebecca to get out of that room. Instead, she took a deep breath and said calmly, "If you don't mind, I'd like to have a room closer to yours."

Rebecca and her father exchanged looks. Vivian held her breath, while the vaporous shadow figure reached a jagged, bone-thin finger toward Rebecca's face and gently stroked her cheek, its bulk still partly obscured by the wall that separated the room from the hallway. Rebecca shifted her gaze to Vivian, unaware of the touch.

Most people never knew the spirits were present. They didn't hear them, they didn't feel them, and they didn't see them like Vivian did. Sometimes Vivian wished she was one of those people. Life would be so much simpler.

"Of course." Rebecca flipped the light off as she stepped out of the doorway. The vapor sucked itself sharply back into the shadows of the room. An unearthly shriek pierced Vivian's ears as Rebecca pulled the door shut behind her.

"We just thought you might like a bit more privacy, but there's a room right next to ours." Rebecca smiled at James as she walked past the stairs where Vivian's body had rooted itself.

Vivian closed her eyes against the high-pitched screeching, as if not seeing would somehow stop her hearing, as well.

"Vivian, are you alright? You're not feeling faint again, are you?" Rebecca asked, pausing at the crest of the staircase.

"No, I'm alright. Just tired."

"We'll get you to your room so you can rest. I'm sure it's been a terribly long day."

Vivian focused her eyes on Rebecca as she moved forward and mounted the landing. It took all of her willpower to keep herself from looking back toward that room.

Somewhere beneath the sound of their footsteps creaking across the floorboards, Vivian thought she heard breathing. The walls around her seemed to be alive, as they pulsated like an asthmatic gasping for air. The hairs on her neck prickled again as the faint sound of claws scraping against wallpaper bled through the walls of the pink bedroom, as if the shadowy figure shut inside was trying to tear through them.

Thane was right; this was an evil spirit. She would definitely avoid it, for now. She had seen enough to understand sadness had a way of making a person vulnerable. And if the spirit knew she could see beyond the living, Vivian feared she might be in danger.

Rebecca chattered on about bedding and wallpaper patterns. She mentioned something about moving a larger dresser from one place to another. Vivian tried to focus on her stepmother's words, nodding occasionally while praying no one else could hear her heart pounding at her chest.

As she entered the bedroom in the far corner of the hallway, the sense of dread that seemed to chase her down the corridor lifted. The tension that stiffened her body eased, and the goose bumps prickling her neck faded.

James placed Vivian's bags on a chaise lounge nestled in a nook by the window. Vivian shut her eyes and listened. A breeze puffed at the leaves in a tree just beyond the window. Peaceful. No screeches. No scratching. No shadows.

Unnerved by what she had just seen only a few yards down the hallway from where she would be sleeping, she began to twist at her hair again.

"I don't think it can leave that room," Thane assured her, startling her with his sudden interjection into her thoughts. *"Hey, you took my bag!"* He was smiling. *"Did you keep Mr. Boo Bear, too?"*

"Of course! And your Yankees hat." Vivian dropped onto the down comforter, too exhausted to stand anymore.

"Thank you, Dad and Rebecca," she said quietly, hoping a few niceties would get them moving toward the door.

"You're welcome, honey." Rebecca smiled.

Vivian wasn't sure she wanted to be called "honey", but she supposed there were worse names her stepmother could call her.

"Can I bring you anything? I've got fresh cookies in the kitchen. You could just crawl into bed, and I could bring some up to you on a tray."

As much as she wanted to hate her stepmother, Vivian was beginning to realize it might be more of an effort to dislike her than she originally thought.

"Yum! Cookies! You should have her whip us up a couple of milkshakes while she's at it!" Thane sprawled out next to Vivian on her bed, his head propped upon his hands. Their father

seemed focused on the spot where he lay.

"No thanks." Vivian peered at her father, wondering why he was looking there. His gaze shifted toward her.

"We'll be right at the end of the hall," he said. He seemed distracted and looked back where Thane sat, a deep crease settled between his eyebrows. "Please, let us know if you need anything at all." His gaze returned to her as he stepped toward her.

She shrank back toward the headboard as he moved closer. *Please don't hug me or kiss me or anything awful like that,* she thought, as the space between them grew smaller.

Seeing her pull away, he straightened his back and gently brushed her hair from her forehead.

"Good night," he whispered as he turned to walk out of the room.

It was then that Vivian saw the small ball of blackness lumped on her father's back. Like a malnourished, black cat clawed into his shoulder. She heard three words hiss almost indiscernibly from the small mass, like a balloon losing air through a tiny hole.

"She hates you."

Usually the dark ones told their hosts lies, but this one spoke the truth. To Vivian, that realization was even more chilling, than seeing the tiny demon riding below the base of her father's neck. It didn't just speak to her father's guilt. It spoke to the darkness that clung to Vivian's own heart.

"Good night, Vivian." Rebecca didn't hesitate to wrap her arms tightly around her stepdaughter's shoulders. Vivian was surprised to find herself hugging back. Rebecca gently kissed her forehead. "Tomorrow will be a better day."

The door clicked shut gently behind her.

Vivian wanted to believe Rebecca's words, but what would be better about tomorrow? Her mother would still be dead. Her father would still be a jerk who didn't care. And her brother would still be a spirit who was by her side one minute and gone the next. Nothing would be better. It would all be just as sucky tomorrow as it was in that very moment.

Thane patted the pillow beside him. *"Try not to think about it all so much."* He smiled that big, dimpled smile he had worn most of his short life. *"We're gonna have a sleep over, just like old times. Only now I can't rip one under the blankets and pull the covers over your head."*

Vivian let herself giggle quietly at the thought as she slipped out of her blue jeans and threw on a pair of gray sweatpants from Thane's duffle bag. It felt good to laugh a little. She pulled her sweatshirt off over her head, leaving on the t-shirt she'd worn underneath, and headed towards the bed.

She paused for a moment by the window, glancing into the darkness behind her new home. The chill of the cool autumn air radiated through the paned glass. For a second, she thought she saw movement through the blur of twisted branches and shadows. Pressing her face against the window, Vivian peered deeper into the darkness, scanning the dense mix of oaks and pines that stretched as far as the darkness would allow her to see. It had probably just been a rabbit or a raccoon scavenging through the thick underbrush, she reasoned.

A gust of wind scraped branches against the side of the house like a desperate creature trying to claw through the walls. Leaves whirled among the thistles and bark. Vivian squinted one last time through the glass. Content there was nothing more than a brisk autumn breeze and nocturnal animal life in the trees, she crossed the room to the nightstand beside her bed and turned on the lamp. She flipped off the overhead light before settling beneath the warmth of the blankets.

"What was that thing in the other room?" she asked Thane, almost too tired to think about it, but too unsettled by its presence to relax completely.

"I'm not sure. I came in ahead to check the place out, and I saw it when I was looking around that room. It chased me, screaming and grabbing at me, but it stopped in the doorway clawing at the air. It must be connected to the room somehow."

"Something awful must have happened in that room."

"Just stay out of there," Thane said firmly.

Although she was disturbed by the idea of such an evil spirit closed away in the bedroom down the hall, Vivian understood something most people didn't. Spirits were always around. She'd started calling the dark ones "shadows" as a young child. And although she'd rather see the spirit of a person who had come to watch over a loved one, she was no more afraid of the dark ones than she was of the ones she called the guardians.

The shadows usually only tormented the person they were attached to. But Vivian understood they preyed on weakness. Her sadness made her vulnerable. So she would stay away from that room, at least for now.

As for the blackness attached to her father's back, he was responsible for that. In her heart she knew her anger would feed it and strengthen the hold it had on her father's spirit. But her emotions were too raw for her to consider the power she had to grow or diminish the demon of regret haunting her father.

Vivian's eyes were too heavy to keep open any longer. She settled her head into the softness of the down pillow, her brother's arm wrapped protectively around her shoulder as he watched the dimly lit room around them. She wasn't sure if it was only in her mind, but she could feel him as if he were flesh and bone. He looked and felt as real as any living person. She could almost forget he was dead. The peacefulness of the room and the comfort of her brother's presence soothed Vivian into a deep, dreamless sleep.

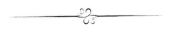

A TWIG SNAPPED UNDER the sole of their shoe. They needed to be quieter, or someone might notice them. The people in the house might look out a window and see them lurking behind the trunk of an oak tree as they watched the girl press her face against the window. Why was she in *that* room? She should have been in the other room. The pink room was meant for her. They stayed a while after the girl turned out her light.

Watching. Breathing with the wind. Waiting.

CHAPTER THREE

SUNLIGHT GLARED THROUGH THE SHEER, WHITE curtain covering the window. A space between the two panels of fabric created a spotlight aimed directly at Vivian's face. Squinting against the harsh light, she shielded herself from the penetrating brightness with her hands. She peeked through fanned fingers and watched dust particles shimmying in the beam of light.

Funny how something that's actually dirt can be so pretty, she thought as her eyes slowly adjusted to the brightness of the morning.

The bed beneath her moaned in protest as Vivian sat up. For a moment, she'd forgotten where she was.

Every morning, she woke up hoping to be back in the crowded bedroom she'd shared with Thane—his stinky shoes laying too close to her bed, their odor welcoming her to a new day. She kept her eyes closed and lay perfectly still, straining to hear the sound of him rolling around on the bunk above her but silence hummed dully in its place.

One day, she might forget the sounds of him rustling in his bed above her in the mornings—the squeak of mattress springs as he rolled from side to side, grunting objections at the alarm clock for disrupting one of his dreams. He seemed to have a good dream every night—the kind where he scored the winning touchdown or kissed the hottest girl in school. It was like God knew his life would be short, so He filled the few dreams Thane would get to have with nothing but the best.

It didn't matter how many times Vivian told him that she did not need to hear every detail of his unconscious fantasies, he shared them anyway. She would trade every good dream she might ever have to hear him tell her about one more of his.

She wondered if she would eventually forget what her own mother's voice sounded like. It had already been so long since she had heard it, that Vivian couldn't quite imagine the exact tone or pitch. She was sure she would know it if she heard it again. But unlike Thane, her mother seemed to be at peace in the place where peaceful spirits depart to when they are content to let life go. One day, her mother's voice would be little more than a pinprick in the tapestry of Vivian's memories. The thought tore at her heart.

Each day greeted her with a new kind of ache—never better or worse than the pain of waking up alone the day before. The realization of another day without her family was nearly as wrenching as losing them all over again.

She let her head drop back onto her pillow and stared at the ceiling. Tears slipped past the corners of her eyes, rolled down her cheeks, and puddled in her ears.

I want to go home, she thought, rubbing at the scar above her eye. It was beginning to throb, and she felt a headache forming behind it.

Slowly, Vivian forced herself to sit up as she swallowed the lump inside her throat. Mushroom-colored walls covered in velvet jacquard floral paper surrounded her.

"My new bedroom is the color of a fungus," she said aloud. "That figures."

She'd been too exhausted the night before to notice much about the aesthetics of her room. This morning, she decided she'd have to ask Rebecca if she could put a few posters on the walls. In its current state, it felt more like a hotel room, than something belonging to a sixteen-year-old girl. She doubted posters would make it feel like home, but it was worth a try.

Slipping into the jeans she'd worn the day before, she grabbed a fresh shirt and Thane's Yankees cap. She breathed deeply through her nose, comforted by the sweaty boy smell still clinging to the hat. Soon that would be gone, too. She wiped at another tear, as it slipped down her cheek.

"Stop being such a baby," Vivian scolded herself, using both hands to shape the bill of the cap above her eyes, as she caught a glimpse of her reflection in the full-length mirror near the window.

Vivian shifted her gaze to the paned-glass window. A canopy of gold and orange covered most of the land behind her room. Pops of red sprinkled in the mix. The combination of colored leaves set on top of the bright green grass below, reminded Vivian of a box of crayons Thane had left in the car one hot summer day, when they were younger. The swirls of colors were so brilliant that her mother had commented on how beautiful they were, as she scrubbed and scraped at the waxy stains left on her upholstery.

"I wish you were here to see this, Thane," she whispered aloud, hoping he'd step out from a corner of her room to announce his presence.

She knew it didn't work that way. The spirits didn't come when she asked them to. They just came, randomly and without warning.

It was the same with the dark spirits. She'd never met anyone who had a shadow hovering over them all the time. They would come and go. They seemed to sense despair, and Vivian had come to believe they drew their strength from hopelessness and sorrow. She didn't understand it all, but she tried to make sense of what she'd seen over the years.

A knock startled her away from her thoughts.

"Vivian?" The door groaned as Rebecca opened it just enough to peek inside. "I'm sorry to bother you, honey."

Ugh – enough with the honey already!

"But I thought you might like to come down and have some breakfast. I've made chocolate chip pancakes. Your dad told me that they're your favorite."

Yeah — they were, when I was like, ten!

Vivian bit the inside of her cheek as she reminded herself that at least Rebecca was trying to be nice and make her feel welcomed. Where was her father? Who cared? It'd be better if he'd just stay away from her altogether.

"Okay. Thanks," she replied with less enthusiasm than she'd intended.

"If you're ready, we can go down to the kitchen together," Rebecca offered brightly, trying to conceal that her feelings had been hurt by Vivian's unenthusiastic response.

"I suppose we'd better go together," Vivian replied, trying to be a bit friendlier. "I might get lost if I try to find it on my own."

"Maybe I should give you a tour of this old place after we eat," Rebecca suggested, as she led Vivian down the hallway. "It can be a bit of a maze."

The house felt much less menacing this morning. And for a moment, Vivian hoped that she might have imagined it all. Maybe the combination of grief, exhaustion, and the apprehension she felt about moving here had somehow made her mind play tricks on her.

The hallway opened to the balcony-like landing at the top of the grand staircase. Sunlight flooded through the oversized windows of the two-story foyer below, casting a warm glow throughout the entire space. Vivian admired the peaceful beauty of it all.

Just a few feet away, the pink bedroom was silent. Its door still closed, just as they'd left it the night before. No unearthly screams. No invisible, beastly claws scratching at the walls.

As they neared the landing, the door to the bedroom just a few feet from her, Vivian was slapped with the unnatural coldness she'd felt before. Something lingered just beyond her perception, something menacing and unearthly, causing goosebumps to spike her flesh. She pressed her knuckle into the scar above her eye, trying to push away the headache that began to pulse behind it.

What could have happened here to cause such a strong spirit to attach itself to that room? Vivian wondered as she descended the stairs behind Rebecca. With her back to the room, the hairs on her neck prickled as a shiver quivered down her spine.

Vivian gazed at the opulent foyer below her—the marble floor, the ornate chandelier—it was like something out of a *Better Homes and Garden* magazine.

How can a place so beautiful hide something so dark?

They made their way through the foyer and down a long, windowless hallway, passing several doors leading off in different directions. Darkness clung to the corners like black cobwebs. The aroma of bacon and hot butter made Vivian's stomach growl with anticipation as she entered the kitchen.

Her father stood at the stove, eggs sizzling on a skillet while a plate of pancakes sat under a warming light. Neatly arranged on a long, wooden table were three place settings. Each complete with a tall glass of milk, a tumbler of orange juice and a cup for coffee.

"Do you drink coffee?" Rebecca asked, as she filled two of the cups from a white carafe.

"Yes, thank you," Vivian lied.

She never drank coffee, but if she put enough cream and sugar in it, it might not be so bad. As she watched steam rise above her freshly-filled cup, Vivian wished she had thought to grab the Snoopy mug her mother had used for her morning coffee. Caressing the chipped handle of her treasured flea market find, her mother would slowly sip her coffee in between questioning Vivian and Thane about their plans for the day.

Her mother's best friend, Jana, had packed up most of the items from the apartment, with the intention of donating them to Goodwill. She had promised to wait a few months before getting rid of anything, to give Vivian some time to decide if there was anything else she wanted to keep. Vivian had told her not to bother—she was sure she'd taken everything that would matter to her. Funny, how little things like coffee mugs seemed important when thinking back on people you've lost. She would have to call Jana and ask her to send the old, chipped mug.

It had always annoyed Vivian that her mother couldn't buy herself nice things. Meanwhile, her father lived in the lap of luxury. Even his new wife was like one of those perfect dolls with the ceramic heads that Vivian had always wanted as a kid, but her mother could never afford. Lips and lashes painted perfectly on creamy porcelain. Exquisite features highlighted by rosy cheeks.

Rebecca positioned a tray of assorted flavored creamers in the center of the table. "I have to load mine up with something sweet." She smiled as she chose a bottle labeled, French Vanilla. "Help yourself, if you'd like."

Vivian poured a large dose of Carmel Latte into her mug. Using the miniature spoon that sat beside her saucer, she swirled the creamy cloud into the blackness of her coffee, creating a tiny funnel in the center of her cup.

Her father carried over a set of plates—one filled with fried eggs and the other chocolate chip pancakes. Swooping in with a dish of bacon, Rebecca bumped James's arm as she placed it on the table. The platter of pancakes wobbled on his palm as he tried to regain control.

Vivian watched, slightly amused, as it slipped from his hand. In one swift motion, Rebecca caught the plate before its load of pancakes spilled on top of the bacon. She had somehow managed to squeeze under James's arm and was pinned between his body and the table.

She laughed, "I can't believe I caught that! That could have been disastrous!" She winked at Vivian. "It's a good thing I have cat-like reflexes, considering what a klutz I am! Sorry I bumped you, babe." She tilted her head and kissed James on the cheek.

"That's alright. Disaster averted." He blushed as he made eye contact with Rebecca.

Vivian watched them as they untangled themselves and sat down. Rebecca sat beside her, and her father settled into a seat across the table. He seemed to be keeping his distance. Vivian was grateful. She had a lot to cope with at the moment, and an overly-affectionate, formerly-prodigal father would only make things worse. But somehow—even though she hated to admit it—there was something comforting about the happiness she sensed between the two of them.

That should have been how you and Mom were together, she thought bitterly. But even as the thought slipped into her mind, she realized that it didn't really matter anymore. Her mother was gone. This pretty blonde who kept calling Vivian "honey" was the closest thing to a mother she had now. Although she hated the thought, she found herself wanting to lay her head on her stepmother's shoulder and sob in the warmth of a hug.

As Vivian finished her second helping of pancakes and bacon, she realized that she hadn't eaten since breakfast the day before. The throbbing above her eye had almost ceased by the time she sopped up all of the extra syrup on her plate with her last bite. She also realized chocolate chip pancakes were still her favorite breakfast food.

Her father set about clearing the plates from the table. Vivian noticed that the shadow creature which had been attached to him last night was gone this morning. She supposed a pleasant family breakfast might have momentarily taken his mind off the fact that his only surviving child wanted nothing to do with him.

As Rebecca stood behind Vivian's chair, she placed a hand gently on her shoulder and said, "Are you ready for the grand tour?"

"Sure," she replied, smiling up at her stepmother. "I could help clean up breakfast, first."

"I've got it under control," her father said. "You girls go ahead."

Rebecca led Vivian through the main level. Vivian was shocked by the aged grandeur and immense size of her new home. She knew it looked large from the outside, but the rooms seemed to link together in an unending labyrinth. A large butler's pantry connected the kitchen to a formal dining room. A parlor opened into a music room, complete with a shiny, black grand piano, which was beautifully framed by a wall of white-paned windows that looked out onto the thick mix of shrubs and trees behind the house.

"There are so many rooms," Vivian said, mostly to herself as they crossed the hallway from the music room into a large office.

"We've been here just over six months, and I'm still trying to get used to having so much space. But I won't complain, as long as I can have Marybeth come a few times a week to help with the cleaning. Can you imagine dusting all of these rooms alone? I'd never do anything else." Rebecca opened a set of French doors.

"This is your father's office," she said, stepping into the room.

A shiny, cherry wood desk centered the room. Angled in one corner of the room was a single leather sofa with rolled arms traced in hammered brass studs. Vivian was surprised to see a bookcase filled with framed photographs of her and Thane lining the wall behind the desk.

"He's able to work from home most days," Rebecca was

saying as she walked noiselessly across a Persian rug, deep-red flowers encased in arcs of gold beneath her feet. "Which is good and bad some days. Especially when he has a conference call or a deadline. Luckily, we've got plenty of room to make ourselves scarce, if we need to."

Rebecca's voice faded into background noise as Vivian gazed over the shelves of photos. Every school picture they'd ever taken was framed and neatly displayed. Scattered between the formal portraits were candid snapshots of happy times. One of the three of them at the fair one summer. Another of them standing in front of the Yankee's stadium, while Thane wore the same hat she was wearing that very moment.

She put one finger gently on his pictured face, as if she might be able to feel the warmth of his skin. The chill of the glass made her shiver.

Her throat tightened as tears threatened to spill from her eyes. She was still scanning the bookshelf, her finger touching Thane's glass-covered image, when Rebecca placed her hand gently on Vivian's back. She didn't say a word, as if she knew there was nothing she could say to make Vivian feel any better. She simply stood beside her and admired the rows of frames with her.

"I remember that day," Vivian spoke quietly as her hand drifted toward a photo of herself and Thane standing on top of a large boulder in front of a waterfall cascading down the side of a steep cliff. "Our hair was wet because we went behind the waterfall. Dad told us there was a cave back there, so we all went through the water to see it."

They'd had to stumble through the rocky riverbed, green and slick with moss, to get to the waterfall. Dad had twisted his ankle, when he'd slipped on the way through the cascading water. Vivian and Thane had helped him down the mountain. He'd joked that it was a preview of what it would be like when he was an old man, his two kids helping him waddle through the halls of the nursing home.

That would never happen. He didn't have two kids anymore. She was the only one left. And she was pretty certain that if he were in need of a helping hand, she'd be the last person to rush to his side.

"Your dad loves these pictures," Rebecca said quietly. "I've looked at them with him and heard the stories so many times that I always felt like I knew you both, even though we'd never met."

Vivian looked at Rebecca, for a moment unable to speak. Why would her dad sit around, reminiscing about a bunch of old pictures? He could have called. She would have laughed about the stories with him. She and Thane could have come to visit. They could have taken more photos. They could have made more memories.

The idea that Thane died thinking their dad hadn't cared about them anymore made Vivian want to scream. The throbbing above her eye returned, as she struggled not to cry hot, angry tears. Slipping the baseball cap off with one hand, she pressed the other palm against the pain as she squeezed her eyes shut.

"Maybe we should get some fresh air," Rebecca suggested.

Vivian nodded, still trying to push away the ache in her forehead with her hand. Silently, they walked together down an unfamiliar hallway and past a large library, a bathroom, and several closed doors Vivian assumed might be closets, or maybe stairwells. Rebecca had mentioned there were two sets of stairs leading to the upper level, and one that led to a basement.

Once outside, Vivian let the cool air blow through her hair as she tilted her head toward the sky. Letting deep breaths fill her lungs, she gazed at wisps of clouds floating slowly above the tree tops.

"There are so many trees around here," she said, awed by

the thick forest in front of her.

"They go on for miles," Rebecca replied. "Our property butts up to a nature preserve about three miles south of where we're standing. Do you like hiking?"

"I used to," Vivian replied. Her headache was fading slowly.

Something rustled behind a bush just a few feet from where she stood. Leaning forward slightly, she squinted toward the movement. A brown rabbit darted into the clearing, thumping toward the cover of a small shrub near the porch. The branches of the bush seemed to swallow him; the white puff of his tail was the last thing to be absorbed by evergreen.

"There's a great area to hike in back here. It's very peaceful."

Vivian scanned the thicket. To her left, the brown shingles of a rooftop peeked above the trees.

"What's that?" she asked, pointing toward the structure.

"That's the groundskeeper's house," Rebecca replied. "Raymond Lowry lives there with his daughter Anna. She's about your age."

Between the main house and the groundskeeper's home was a smaller rooftop, barely visible above the tree line.

"What's the smaller building?" Vivian asked.

"The old coal shed. I've been asking your father to have it torn down since the day we moved in. It's nearly falling apart anyway, and I'm pretty sure coal heat isn't a trend that's coming back."

"Rebecca!" Vivian's father suddenly appeared on the veranda waving a black cordless phone in his hand. "It's Paula."

"I'm sorry, Vivian. I better take this. Somehow I got suckered into heading up the church fundraising committee, and if Paula's calling, it can only mean one thing...dissension in the ranks." She winked and hustled toward the phone.

"Hey, Paula," she said, cupping the phone against her ear as she disappeared into the house.

Her father stepped down from the porch and stood near Vivian. "I can walk with you and finish showing you around," he offered with a hesitant yet hopeful smile. His pale blue eyes were almost pleading.

Vivian was not about to give him the satisfaction of being her buddy. "I think I'd like to check it out on my own," she replied turning away from him.

Even as the words slipped out of her mouth, she could see a thin sliver of darkness snake across the grass. It seemed as if it had been hiding in her own shadow, cast from the steadily rising sun before slithering away from her and up her father's leg. The demon of regret crawled up her father's back before settling into a small, black mass upon his shoulder.

She walked across the yard and into the trees, refusing to look back. Tangles of twigs and bark shrouded her from the sad stare of her father. When she finally turned around, the yard behind her was empty.

Good, she thought bitterly. *I'd rather be alone in the middle of nowhere, than around him!*

CHAPTER FOUR

VIVIAN WAS COMPLETELY SURROUNDED BY TREES. She stood in the silence of their unmoving branches. The wind that had raged against their limbs the night before had calmed, and the air was completely still. It should have felt peaceful, to stand in the beauty of the fall colors bathed in sunshine, but in the stillness, Vivian was unsettled by the feeling that she wasn't alone.

Moving deliberately across the layers of dead leaves and broken twigs, Vivian looked around the tree trunks. She almost expected to see someone, maybe the groundskeeper or his daughter, clearing out the underbrush or taking a late morning stroll.

As far as she could see, she was alone. But the sense that someone was watching her caused a nervous knot to twist inside her stomach. Maybe her father was still out back, keeping an eye on her to make sure she didn't wander too far.

She turned around and squinted through the hanging branches toward the house. The yard was empty.

Scanning the steep pitches of the roofline along the back of the house, sprouts of English Ivy creeping up the tan brick exterior, Vivian noticed movement in one of the upstairs windows. Her gaze had passed by the windows so quickly that she wasn't sure which room she'd seen it in. As she looked over the windows more slowly, a gasp tangled in her throat. Half hidden by the folds of sheer white fabric in her bedroom window stood a figure, gazing down at her.

"It must be Rebecca or my dad," she tried to reason as she released an unsteady breath. She smiled uncomfortably, wondering why either of them would be in her room, and waved.

The figure in the window did not move. It stood eerily still, staring back at her. Vivian squinted as she tried to see more clearly who was there, but branches blocked her line of sight, and the sheer fabric hid the details of the face.

Just then, she heard her father and Rebecca speaking to each other. Turning her gaze in the direction of their voices, she saw both of them walking toward her through the trees. As she looked back at her window, Vivian froze. Her heart thumped wildly against her chest when she saw the figure was still watching her.

Slowly a hand rose up behind the sheer fabric with one finger pointed at her. The finger moved deliberately toward an obscured face and rested in front of a mouth veiled by the thin curtain. She could almost hear the "*shh*" as a lump rose in her throat, pressing out the scream that had settled there.

"Dad! Rebecca!" she shouted frantically running toward them. "Someone is in my bedroom!"

Her legs could not keep up with her body as she stumbled through the trees. She tripped over a fallen branch and twisted her ankle. Pain shot through her calf like a hot blade as she tried to stand. Her father moved quickly through the underbrush and knelt beside her.

"Are you hurt?" he asked breathlessly.

"Oh, honey! Are you okay?" Rebecca said stooping beside her husband.

Vivian grimaced as she tried to put her weight onto her injured ankle and stand. She crumpled back onto the forest floor.

Placing a hand on her shoulder, her father calmly said, "Don't move. It could be broken. Just stay still and let me look at it."

"But there's someone in my room!" Vivian's voice cracked as she yelled. "They were watching me!"

Rebecca stood and looked up at Vivian's bedroom window. "I don't see anyone." She ran a few yards back toward the house.

"Raymond!" Rebecca shouted through cupped hands.

A man came around the corner of the house. "Yes, Mrs. Bennett." he said, catching his breath. A girl around Vivian's age soon appeared behind him, holding a rake in one hand.

"Vivian thinks she saw someone in her room. Were you or Anna in the house?"

"No, Ma'am! We were in the front, raking leaves in the yard."

"Someone was there, standing behind the curtain," Vivian insisted, heat rising into her cheeks. She grimaced at the searing pain that shot through her ankle.

"Vivian, there's no one else on the property. Are you sure you saw someone?" Rebecca questioned, walking toward the house as she stared up toward the bedroom. The curtains hung motionless. In the corner of the window nook stood the swivel mirror Vivian had dressed in front of that morning. "Maybe it was just the mirror you saw."

"They pointed at me," Vivian said looking into her father's eyes, pleading with him to believe her.

"Raymond, would you mind looking around inside, just to make sure no one's there?" he asked, keeping eye contact with Vivian as he spoke.

"Dad, someone *was* there. You have to believe me!"

"I do believe you, Vivian. Let me get you inside so we

can look at your ankle. We'll figure out what's going on." He slipped his arms under her body and cradled her as he walked with smooth, steady strides toward the house. The small shadowy clump that had been on his shoulder earlier was gone, for the moment. Vivian wrapped her arms around his neck to steady herself in his grasp.

For a moment she felt like a little girl. For a moment he felt like her daddy again. She closed her eyes against the pain—the physical hurt of her twisted ankle and the aching need to love the man she was certain she'd hate forever.

James laid Vivian on the same sofa she had passed out on the night before. Meanwhile, Rebecca rushed though the room with an icepack and pressed it gently against Vivian's throbbing ankle. The girl, Anna, stood in the doorway between the foyer and the sitting room, as if passing over the threshold might cause her to spontaneously combust.

"I'm going upstairs to help Raymond search the house," her father said firmly as he crossed the room. Using a key that hung on a hook inside a bookcase, he opened a wooden box. Vivian wasn't sure what he was getting until she heard the jingle of lead against metal as he placed bullets into the chamber of a handgun.

He does believe me, she thought as he strode across the room and took the stairs in the foyer two at a time.

"Anna, could you help Vivian hold this icepack while I find something to wrap her ankle with?" Rebecca was already out of the room before Anna could respond.

The girl moved quickly to Vivian's side and smiled down at her, as she placed the ice on her ankle. "I'm Anna." Her voice was barely more than a whisper.

"I'm Vivian."

"I know." Her smile faded. "I'm really sorry about your mom and brother."

For a moment Vivian thought Anna might cry. Somehow, in that one sentence, Vivian got the sense that Anna could actually understand Vivian's loss. So many others had given her condolences after the accident, but most of them felt awkward, almost as if they said it simply because it was the polite thing to say. But Vivian had the sense Anna somehow shared her sadness.

"Thanks," she replied quietly.

James walked briskly into the sitting room with Raymond just steps behind.

"There's no one in the house other than us," he said to Rebecca as she entered the room through a side door, leading to what Vivian thought she remembered to be a formal dining room. "We looked everywhere, even the attic and the basement."

Vivian was glad they hadn't found someone lurking around the house. But worry twisted through her relief the way the cream had swirled into her coffee that morning. She had seen someone in her bedroom; she was certain of that. Or maybe it was something. Maybe the shadow from the pink room could move freely through the house.

Her mind whirled, as she tried to imagine every possible explanation for what she had seen—a guardian spirit, the shadow spirit she'd seen the night before, or maybe a different shadow. She was sure it wasn't Thane. He wouldn't try to scare her. There was something menacing about the way the figure had looked at her. The thought made a shiver run up her spine.

Rebecca sat on the edge of the sofa. "Honey, it's been such a long couple of days. You must be so tired. Do you think you might have imagined seeing someone?" she asked in a soothing tone, as she gingerly wrapped Vivian's ankle.

"I suppose, I might have," Vivian lied. She wasn't sure exactly what she had seen, but she was sure that she hadn't imagined any of it. But if no *person* was in the house, it must have been a spirit. It would be better to let them think she was going crazy than to tell them she was able to see the spirits.

"I haven't been sleeping well since..." Her unfinished sentence hung tangled in the air.

"I understand," Rebecca replied as she finished wrapping her injured ankle. Vivian stood up slowly. The dull throbbing radiating through her ankle balanced out the headache that once again knocked behind her forehead. She slipped off Thane's baseball cap and pressed her palm against her scar as it pulsed with pain.

"I think I'd like to get some fresh air," she said limping toward the foyer.

"I'll go with her," Anna offered, settling the worried looks exchanged between everyone in the room. "If you don't mind company," she interjected, smiling kindly at Vivian.

"No, actually a tour guide would be great." She felt herself brighten up at the prospect of spending time with someone her own age.

The girls headed out the front door. To someone looking at them from behind, they could have passed as twins. Their hair, the same golden shade of brown, swayed loosely at the center of their backs. Both were thinly built and nearly the same height.

As they explored the property together, the stiffness in Vivian's ankle began to fade. She felt an immediate friendship as they laughed, and she watched Anna chase kittens through the hay bales in the barn, trying to catch one for Vivian to hold.

"The house was built over a hundred and twenty years ago," Anna said, gently stroking a tabby kitten in her lap. The mother cat purred quietly as it circled Vivian, rubbing the sides of her back against the girl's wrapped ankle. She reached down and gently stroked the cat behind its ears.

"The Lowry's have been the groundskeepers since it was built. My great-great-great grandfather actually helped pour the concrete for the foundation."

"Wow," Vivian replied. "That's really cool!"

"My dad remembers when the tunnel was open between the coal shed and the main house. He loves to tell me stories about hiding out in there when he was a kid."

"You mean there's actually an underground passageway between the house and the shed?" Vivian asked in disbelief.

"Yeah, but your father had it bricked up after he moved in. The shed is pretty rickety, and your dad has asked my dad to take it down and fill in the tunnel all together."

"Ah, that's sort of a shame." Vivian smiled before shrugging her shoulders. "Although I'm sort of glad it's blocked off. The idea of an underground tunnel is a little...creepy."

"Yeah, I never really thought about it. It's just always been there, and I've just always been *here*. Four generations of my family were born in my house. I would have been the fifth, only my mother insisted on having me at a hospital."

Anna paused as she reached down to pet the mother cat. "My dad's hoping I'll marry some strapping young handyman one day and keep the tradition going," Anna said, her voice trailed off as she looked absently across the barn.

"What are you hoping for?"

Anna continued to gaze across the bales of hay. For a moment, Vivian wondered if she had heard her question. Then Anna turned her gaze toward Vivian.

"College. Maybe somewhere out of state." She shrugged her shoulders as she stroked the mother cat who had curled up contently on her lap. "Sometimes I think it would be nice to get away from here."

"Yeah," Vivian laughed. "I've only been around a day, and I'm already dying to get out of here!"

"I suppose it's really different from the city."

"I feel like I'm on an entirely different planet!" Vivian replied, picking up the mother cat. A wet nose tickled her neck as the feline stood on Anna's lap and pressed its head against her chin. Vivian giggled. "Although I suppose it's not a bad planet to visit for a while."

"Wait until you get to school tomorrow."

"Is it small?"

"We only needed one school bus for last year's sophomore field trip, and we didn't even fill it up."

"Seriously?" Vivian's eyes widened as she shook her head in disbelief.

"One good thing is you get to know everyone in your class. They say the nice thing about a small town is that when you're not sure what you're doing, someone else can tell you. That's pretty much true at our school."

"Great. I can't wait," Vivian replied with mock enthusiasm. "My mom grew up in a small town. She liked to say, 'My hometown was so small, you couldn't fart without everybody knowing about it.'"

"Your *mom* would say that?" Anna chuckled.

"My mom was never short on interesting and embarrassing things to say." Vivian ran her hand across the soft fur of the cat as it traveled between her lap and Anna's, the gentle trill of her purr filling the few moments of silence following Vivian's words.

"The good news is, we'll be able to find each other tomorrow. It's not like you'll get lost in the crowd!"

Vivian was grateful she would at least know someone at school. Though she hated to admit it, she was nervous about being the new kid. At least now she wouldn't feel completely alone.

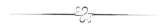

THEY WATCHED HER LAUGHING in the barn. Tingles of excitement ran through their body. She was so pretty when she smiled—so very pretty. She wasn't supposed to see them watching her from the window earlier. They didn't want to scare her. Not yet, anyway. That time would come soon enough.

She was different than the girls they'd watched before. It was as if she could sense their presence even when they were hiding so well. Their breath came in staggered, jagged gulps. They had to be more careful if they wanted things to go as planned.

CHAPTER FIVE

"YOU'LL HAVE TO TAKE THAT SEAT in the back row," Mr. Wesley said, pointing toward the only empty seat in the room.

"Okay," Vivian smiled weakly. She walked slowly toward the back of the room and slipped into the chair, sandwiched between two other students. The twig-thin boy to her left glanced at her with bulging eyes that were magnified by the thick lens of his plastic-framed glasses. She shifted uncomfortably in her seat and smiled at him as he looked at her with a blank stare, crinkling his nose as if smelling a fart. He shifted his attention back to a scab he'd been picking at on the back of his hand.

I don't even want to know what he's going to do with that thing when he scratches it off. Vivian thought, trying not to gag as she watched in disgust.

Deciding it was better to look away and pretend she wasn't sitting beside the token scab-picker, she turned to look at the girl on her right. The girl's dyed, black hair hung around the sides of her face like a curtain. She peered at Vivian from behind blue tipped bangs that touched the tops of her eyelashes. Her lipstick was almost as dark as her hair.

"He eats them," she said, pulling a hidden set of ear buds from behind her hair.

"What?"

"Yeah, picks 'em off and sticks 'em right in his mouth."

"Disgusting."

"He tried to touch me with one once, but I punched him in the junk, and he hasn't done it since."

Vivian peered over her shoulder at her scab-eating neighbor. Now it was her turn to crinkle her nose in disgust. She recoiled, as he looked up from his work and smiled mischievously at her.

"If you try that crap on her, Harry, I'll punch ya' in the junk, again." The girl glared at the boy, squinting her eyes, thickly rimmed with black liner. "His name's Harry Crap, no joke! It's like his parents wanted him to get his butt kicked every day!"

"No kidding?" Vivian shifted herself to the edge of her chair, as far away as possible from the boy who appeared to live up to the disgusting name he'd been cursed with. Her shoulder pressed against the black sweatshirt of the girl beside her. "Hey, thanks." She smiled. "I'm Vivian."

"I'm Jen. No sweat," she said shrugging her shoulders. She slipped her ear buds back in, as the hair curtain closed around her face.

Jen wouldn't have been the first person Vivian would have tried to befriend, but she was the only person who didn't fall within the age bracket to qualify for the early bird special at IHOP to speak to Vivian all day. Being acknowledged by someone her own age made her feel human.

Vivian slumped slightly in her seat, as Mr. Wesley instructed the class to open their notebooks and ready their pens. She scribbled notes as her new history teacher yammered on about slavery.

Even Mr. Wesley's enthusiasm for the subject couldn't capture her attention for more than a few moments. Before long, her eyes wandered around the room, observing her new classmates scribbling notes or gazing ahead in various stages of boredom.

She hadn't noticed Jen's shadow figure right away. It was almost as cloaked by her dark clothes and hair as she was. Vivian might not have noticed it at all, if she hadn't heard it whispering.

"You're no good," it rasped in a voice almost as light as a breeze. *"Worthless. Ugly. Fat. Even your own mother hates you."*

Vivian wanted to stick up for the girl. She fought the urge to tell the shadow to go back to hell and leave Jen alone! She wished she could threaten to punch *it* in its junk, if it had any, just as Jen had stuck up for her. But she was afraid to let the shadows know she could see them.

She'd never worried much about it before the accident, but she'd been mostly happy then. Sure, there was the whole abandoned-by-her-father thing, but she dealt with her anger over that issue pretty well.

She was a girl with lots of friends. She was a girl who got asked out on dates by boys, and had even had a steady boyfriend, for a while. But she wasn't that girl anymore. Now she was sad, and angry, and lost, and bitterly lonely. She worried the shadows would sense her pain and one of them might attach itself to her.

Jen looked up from the doodle she'd been laboring over throughout the lecture. She held up her notebook, and proudly flashed Vivian the picture she'd sketched of Mr. Wesley, wearing a loin cloth and swinging from a vine like some middle-aged, beer-bellied Tarzan with a history book clutched in one hand. Vivian stifled a giggle and gave Jen an enthusiastic thumbs-up.

Setting down her notebook, Jen continued to scribble at the page. With her elbows propped on the tabletop, Vivian rested her chin in the palms of her hands and continued gazing around the room.

One boy, apparently a football player, judging from the red jersey numbered eighteen draped over his back, sat with his head down on the table. A black vapor hovered behind his left shoulder, suspended, unmoving. It seemed to be napping with him.

Vivian had been able to see the spirits attached to her classmates as long as she could remember. The first shadow spirit she could recall was attached to Maggie Fraiser, when they were in kindergarten. Maggie always wore long sleeves, even when the temperatures in the school made other children peel off their sweatshirts. In late September of second grade, Maggie moved away. She had gone to live with relatives. Years later, Vivian's mother told her that Maggie had been removed from her home because her father was abusing her.

By middle school, a handful of her classmates had shadows because they were experimenting with drugs or alcohol. Others struggled with the shadows of depression. By the time she'd entered high school, the ratio of shadows to students was fairly high.

Her ability to see the dark spirits linked to others had taught her at an early age that life was difficult and sad for many people. Even the kids who outwardly seemed to have it all together were often tormented by the unseen beings, poisoning their minds with hurtful words and sad thoughts.

Vivian couldn't help but wonder what number eighteen's story was. He seemed to be one of the more popular kids at Richfield High.

She had noticed him before school in the commons that morning, a cheerleader flanked on both sides. A group of football players shouted around him. It was a sea of red jerseys and pleated cheer skirts. A smile had parted his lips, revealing perfectly straight teeth. His right cheek dimpled as he laughed. It was like a scene from a cheery, teen sitcom, except for the shadow peeking over his thick, muscular shoulder.

Mr. Wesley's voice grew louder and higher pitched as he discussed the deplorable conditions endured by imprisoned slaves on the Middle Passage.

"Slaves on the boats crossing the Atlantic Ocean succumbed to disease because of the human defecation aboard the ship. Many threw themselves into the frigid waters— certain death as the heavy chains and shackles that bound their legs pulled them below the waves to the ocean floor."

I wish I could jump off the ship I'm on, Vivian mused miserably.

She could almost imagine Mr. Wesley bursting into tears if he continued the lecture. But his passionate discourse was interrupted when a wadded-up ball of paper sailed from the back row of tables and slapped the back of number eighteen's head.

The boy bolted upright, wiping at drool that had seeped from the corner of his mouth during his mid-class slumber.

"Welcome back, Grant! I didn't realize the plight of West African slaves could induce such a peaceful sleep." Mr. Wesley's voice was calm, yet mocking.

"Sorry, sir," the boy responded respectfully. "I guess I didn't sleep very well last night."

"He gets all uptight when we have a big game, Mr. W.," chirped another boy in a red jersey, numbered twenty-three.

"Thank you for your invaluable insight, Jason." Mr. Wesley smirked. "I suppose being the starting quarterback could induce a little pregame anxiety."

"Yes, sir. I'm really sorry," replied Grant. He glanced behind him, scanning the rows of faces for any signs of guilt. When his eyes caught Vivian's, he smiled. She smiled back, trying to keep her eyes on those flawless teeth or that deep dimple—anything to avoid looking at the plume of black hovering beside him.

When the bell rang, Grant was still smiling at Vivian. He watched her with a goofy grin, until one of the cheerleaders

Vivian had seen standing beside him that morning jabbed him in the ribs with a pencil.

"Careful, Hailey," Jason teased. "We need our man injury-free before he steps onto the field."

The girl accosting Grant shot a dirty look at Vivian. Hailey's long, blond hair bounced on top of her head in a ponytail, secured with red, black, and silver ribbon. Her glossed lips curled into an all-too-sweet smile.

"Time for lunch," she said cheerfully, trying—and failing—to conceal the jealousy that tugged at her vocal chords. Her exaggerated grin and overly enthusiastic voice couldn't camouflage the dark, misty creature that had begun to materialize beside her, whispering feverishly into her ear.

Grant turned his attention to the cute cheerleader next to him and followed her out the door. Vivian saw him glance over his shoulder at her as he turned down the hallway.

Tugging the strap of her backpack over her shoulder, Vivian followed the flood of bodies toward the cafeteria. The lunchroom smells mingled together, making it impossible to pinpoint an exact aroma. It was a mixture of over-salted food laden with too much grease, but somehow the rather unappetizing combination made Vivian's stomach rumble. She had been too anxious to eat breakfast that morning, even though Rebecca had greeted her in the kitchen with another round of chocolate chip pancakes.

"Eat up! You'll need your energy for your first day at school," her stepmother had instructed.

But the few bites Vivian had managed to swallow seemed to stick in her throat. She washed them down with coffee which was more white chocolate mocha creamer than actual coffee. After Vivian had picked at the pancakes and rearranged them on the plate, Rebecca had narrowed her eyes from across the table.

"I have a nervous stomach," Vivian admitted.

"You'll fit right in," Rebecca had assured her. Her smile

had been so warm, her words so full of enthusiasm, that Vivian had almost believed her. At least for a moment.

The memory of Rebecca's words seemed funny as Vivian looked at the crowd of students milling around her. She felt the exact opposite of fitting in. She felt more like a "turd in a punchbowl," as her mother had been so fond of saying. While not exactly an eloquent analogy, it seemed to describe her current situation rather well.

She fell in tow with the students moving through the lunch line, holding out teal trays as elderly women, wearing white jackets and hairnets, scooped and ladled various portions of a well-rounded lunch into the assorted squares and rectangles on their trays—a mound of instant mashed potatoes buried under a puddle of turkey gravy, limp green beans, and fruit cocktail with cubes of peaches, pears, and grapes that might have once been green. Vivian scanned the tables beyond the serving line, as she placed a carton of skim milk in her last empty square.

Beads of perspiration began to form on her forehead as she wondered where she would sit. Last night, Anna had promised to save her a spot at her table *if* they had the same lunch period. Vivian wondered if anyone would be nice enough to invite her to sit with them if Anna wasn't there. Considering the only human interaction she'd had all day had been teachers directing her to assigned seats and Jen's brief, yet brash expression of kindness, she doubted there'd be a welcoming committee for her at lunch.

The same anxious knot that had made her unable to eat breakfast that morning, returned as she made her way through the crowd. She was just about to reach an empty table by the back wall when a pack of rowdy boys filled the benches, their trays clattering as they squeezed their long legs and growing bodies into the small space between the bench and the table. They looked awkwardly pinched into the seats, almost like grown men trying to fit onto chairs in a kindergarten classroom.

A group of sufficiently enthusiastic cheerleaders selling homecoming tickets greeted students as they entered the cafeteria. She scanned the blur of bodies and unfamiliar faces, wondering if she should have bypassed the cafeteria altogether and hid out in the girls' locker room for the thirty minute lunch break.

The cute blonde from her last class peered at Vivian as she talked rapidly to the girl standing next to her. With their short skirts, matching RHS windbreakers, and blond hair pulled high on their heads with identical ribbons, Vivian wondered if they might be sisters. Both girls smiled as they stared, but it didn't feel like a friendly "we want to be your friend" kind of smile.

Number eighteen joined them on the other side of the table. He glanced over his shoulder toward Vivian before returning his gaze to Hailey, nodding his head, and speaking words that Vivian could only wonder about.

As she looked away from the homecoming table and gazed through the cafeteria, resuming her mission to find a place to sit, she came to the uncomfortable realization that most of the people in the room were looking at her. Even the small group of teachers huddled near the trophy case seemed interested in her next move.

"…I'm sure it's hair extensions…"

"…she's probably had a nose job, too!"

Were they seriously talking about her? She could never have afforded hair extensions. And if this was a nose job, she wanted her money back!

"…just because her dad's loaded…"

"…thinks she's cool because she's from a big city…"

Suddenly the thin, plastic tray she was holding felt like a platter full of bricks. Her arms began to shake, and she was sure her legs had become rooted to the beige tile under her feet. Just as she began to think her best option was to empty her tray in the trash and wait out lunch in the locker room, she saw Anna waving at her.

"Vivian, over here!" she shouted, her voice rising above the casual chitchat and muttered speculations of the students around her.

Vivian fought the urge to run to Anna and tried to be casual as her feet drug across the floor. With each step, she worried her knees might actually lock, rendering her frozen again. Or worse, they might buckle beneath her and send her toppling over. She'd never been a fan of being the center of attention, and the sudden lull in chatter made her even more aware of the curious glances from her peers.

"I saved a spot for you," Anna said, motioning toward the open bench beside her.

Vivian was relieved when she finally squeezed between Anna and another girl.

"Thanks," she smiled. "I was beginning to think I might have to sit at the homecoming table with the cheerleaders."

"They'd probably stick you in a pleated skirt and toss you on the top of a human pyramid." A lanky boy flashed a crooked smile at her, as he brushed his ink black hair away from his eyes.

"A mistake they'd regret, once they realized how uncoordinated I am." Vivian forced a laugh, trying to sound casual.

"We can't let the cheerleaders get a hold of you," added the girl next to Vivian. "They'll suck your brain out and replace it with a microchip. You'll only be able to recite cheers and the school song. And your phone number so you can give it out to the muscle-heads!"

"Oh, stop it, Tori!" Anna laughed. "I was a cheerleader last year!" She spooned up a bite of mashed potatoes and gravy. "And they don't suck out all of your brain, just part of it! Lucky for me, it regenerates!"

"Kind of like how my gecko grew a new tail after my

little brother pulled the other one off. Only the new one was all lumpy and weird," the boy teased.

"Yeah, Zack, exactly like that!" Anna crossed her eyes and grinned a Mad-Hatter-style smile.

Vivian felt the tension in her muscles ease as she laughed through lunch with Anna and her friends. For half an hour, she almost felt "normal" again. She wasn't the weird new girl who might as well have dropped from the sky for all the strange glances and whispered words she endured. She wasn't even the girl who's mom and brother had died before her eyes. She was just a sixteen-year-old girl, laughing with other kids about normal stuff. Normal felt nice. She had missed it.

Too bad, it was a fleeting feeling. Her tray clattered noisily onto the metal counter top at the tray return window, as another hair-netted woman cheerfully told her to have a good day.

That is not even remotely possible, she thought as she swam upstream with the other kids heading toward fifth period.

Most of the afternoon blurred past. More stares. Very little conversation, other than, "You can take the empty seat in the back." Or, "You'll need to read chapters one through six to catch up." There was plenty of conversation *about* her, which she tried to tune out. She wasn't bold enough to set anyone straight. Maybe she would have been a month ago, but this was not her life anymore. It was someone else's life. And she was just a passenger along for the miserable ride.

She breathed a sigh of relief when she realized she had finally made it to the last class of the day. Passing through the cafeteria, she headed toward the gymnasium for her eighth period, P.E. class. A quartet of girls walked in a huddle ahead of her.

"No way! Mr. Jackson does not have a cute butt!" the redhead protested, crinkling up the freckles on her nose. "That's just gross, Clare!"

"He totally does," another chirped. "You could definitely

bounce a quarter off that thing!"

"Why would anyone want to bounce a quarter off a butt?" the redhead mused. She appeared to be taking the statement literally as one eyebrow raised in contemplation.

"Geeze, Emily! It's just an expression!"

"Maybe," chimed another, "but I'd sure like to try!"

The group erupted into a chorus of giggles as a tall, muscular teacher came out of the doorway labeled, "Physical Education".

"Afternoon, ladies," he said casually.

"Hi, Mr. Jackson," they managed to chime in unison, before another round of giggles shook through their bodies.

The group of snickering girls turned to watch Mr. Jackson as he casually walked around the corner and into the gymnasium. Their gazes quickly shifted toward Vivian.

"Hi," said the thinnest girl. Her chocolate-brown hair was swept to one side in a loose braid. "I'm Clare. This is Emily, Tasha, and Gia." She motioned toward each girl as she mentioned their names.

Vivian hadn't spoken for so long, she almost couldn't find her voice. "Hi," her voice crackled as she cleared the cobwebs that had settled in her throat. "I'm Vivian."

"We know." Tasha smiled.

"Everyone knows who you are." Gia winked. "Heck, the way people talk around here, we probably know stuff about you that you don't even know!"

"I wouldn't doubt that." Vivian laughed.

"Girls, locker room. Now!" A fit woman, who appeared to be in her early thirties's came out of the P.E. office holding a pair of red shorts and a matching red shirt. "You must be the new girl." She half-smiled at Vivian. "These are for you." She thrust the clothes and a small padlock towards Vivian and began walking toward the gymnasium. "Pick a locker without a lock on it. The combo's on the sticky note, stuck to the lock. If you don't hurry up and get changed, you'll be counted tardy," she said, not looking back.

So the girls' gym teacher wasn't a warm fuzzy, but what had Vivian expected? So far, warm fuzzies didn't seem to be the norm at her new school.

She changed into the polyester gym shorts as quickly as she could, but struggled to make her padlock work. By the time she slipped into the gym, Mr. Jackson was already giving directions.

"We'll practice volleying the ball back and forth over the net." His voice boomed through the gymnasium and rattled in Vivian's head. "Partner up."

Students swarmed around, each picking someone to complete their pair, then spread out opposite their partner at the mesh nets. Soon, Vivian stood alone, as volleyballs slapped skin and zipped through the musty air. Just as she realized there was no one left to be her partner, number eighteen ran into the gym, only he was wearing blue shorts and a matching shirt.

"Hey, Mr. J!" he smiled. "Coach grabbed me in the hall."

"No problem, Grant. Looks like we've got a partner for ya right here." He patted Vivian on her thin shoulder, nearly knocking her over.

Vivian thought for a moment that he actually looked happy to be paired up with her but quickly chalked it up as wishful thinking. With the volleyball nestled between his sculpted bicep and thick chest, Grant reached his right hand toward Vivian. "Hey, I'm Grant."

Vivian gazed at his gorgeous smile. Any reply she might have thought to utter was lost somewhere between her brain and her mouth. For a moment, she felt as if he might have somehow managed to hypnotize her with his perfect teeth. She was relieved to see he was alone; his shadow figure was nowhere around.

Vivian had observed over the years how the spirits came and went. They seemed to mostly manifest themselves when people were struggling with self-doubt or depression. Some people unknowingly wore their dark shadows all the time, likely because their self-esteem was in a chronically low place. While others seemed to be able to shake off the sadness or worry, and at the same time, without knowing it, also shook off the dark entity that clung to them.

After a slightly awkward pause, she realized he wanted to shake her hand, which suddenly felt damp with sweat. She wiped it on the side of her shorts and extended her arm timidly.

"I'm Vivian."

His grasp was firm, but gentle. His blue eyes looked straight into hers, as he confidently said, "Welcome to Richfield High! Hope your first day hasn't been too painful."

"I suppose that would depend on your threshold for pain." She smiled feeling less sure of herself than her voice sounded. He laughed.

"You'll have to take the net in the corner!" Mr. Jackson shouted, clearly wanting them to get started.

Her shoulder bumped his as they walked side-by-side toward the only open net, tucked in the far corner of the gym. Her body tingled as if she were somehow charged with electricity.

As they stood close to the net, they tapped the ball back and forth.

"I think we have four classes together." He smiled while he gently pushed the ball off the tips of his fingers.

"Hmm…I noticed you in fourth. And of course, now. What other classes?"

"First and seventh. I kind of hide out in the back of the room in those classes." The ball sailed over his head, and he spun around to grab it as it rolled across the floor. Vivian couldn't help smiling as he bent over to pick it up.

Not a bad view from behind, number eighteen.

"I've kind of been on autopilot today. I probably

wouldn't have noticed if Mrs. Singer had taught the entire seventh hour in the buff."

Laughing, Grant raised an eyebrow, tossed the ball above his head and slapped it with his palm. "She's like a hundred. I think you'd probably notice that!"

"I don't know. I'm pretty out of it today." She bent her knees and bumped the ball back. He returned it with a soft set.

"It's gotta be rough—going to a new school."

Bump. Set. Bump. Set.

"Yeah, it's weird. And I get the feeling that Richfield hasn't seen a new kid in a while."

"Not since Brady McEnroe came midyear in second grade."

Set. Set. Bump.

"For real? No wonder everyone looks at me like I'm an alien!"

"I was going to ask what planet you were from, but maybe you don't want to talk about it." He laughed, winking at her while they volleyed the ball back and forth.

She wasn't sure, but it felt like they were flirting. She couldn't help but think that the blonde from fourth period would probably go into hysterics seeing him wink at her.

With a single blast from Mr. Jackson's whistle, the sound of palms slapping leather stopped, and all eyes turned to face the center of the gym.

"Balls in the carts! Shower up, and don't forget to cheer the Bulldogs on to victory tonight out on the football field!" His voice bounced off the high ceiling and vibrated in Vivian's ears.

"Yo, Grant! Let's make a burger run immediately after school." Number twenty-three slapped his palm onto Grant's shoulder, before extending it toward Vivian. "I'm Jason Bashly, President of the welcoming committee."

Grant rolled his eyes and shook his head with a small smile as Vivian shook Jason's hand.

"I'm Vivian," she said.

"Please, let me know if you need anything at all to make your transition to Richfield High a smooth one," he continued in an exaggeratedly official voice.

"Pleasure to meet you, Mr. President." Vivian played along.

"The pleasure is all mine." Jason grinned.

"If *you* don't leave, I can't leave," Mr. Jackson shouted across the gym.

"T-minus five to burger time," Jason said to Grant as he began to walk backwards toward the doorway. "See ya around, Vivian." He nodded with a friendly smile, before turning and hustling out of the gymnasium.

"There is no welcoming committee," Grant whispered.

"I figured," Vivian whispered back.

"Are you coming to the game tonight?" Grant asked.

"No. I mean, I don't think so. I don't really have anyone to go with."

"Oh." He looked down at his shoe while he squeaked his heel into the maroon center court line beneath his feet.

"Well, I'll see you around," he said looking up at her. His eyes seemed to twinkle in the fluorescent glow of the overhead lights.

Vivian thought he looked disappointed. No. He wouldn't care if she went to the football game. She decided she was just wishing he were disappointed, maybe because she was, a little. It would be fun to sit in the stands and watch number eighteen run around on the field in his spandex football pants.

She smiled, imagining it as she watched him jog across the gym and drop the ball into the ball cart. When he reached the double doors he stopped, turned to look at Vivian one last time, and smiled before disappearing into the hallway.

"You better be careful," Clare said, snapping Vivian away from her thoughts of cute butts in tight pants and back into the musty gymnasium.

"What do you mean?" she asked, genuinely confused.

"His girlfriend would freak if she saw you guys talking like that," Emily replied, her red hair bobbing around her pudgy cheeks.

"Yeah," Gia chimed in. "Hailey would lose it if she knew you were flirting with Grant!"

"Since when is talking to a boy a crime?" Vivian asked defensively. "Besides, I don't think being stuck together by the gym teacher actually qualifies as a date, so I think you guys should just relax." She felt herself bristle as the four girls who'd introduced themselves in the hallway stared back at her. For several long seconds, the buzz from the overhead lights was the only sound.

"Look, we're just warning you," Tasha said as she smiled uncomfortably. She looked around the gym as if someone might be hiding behind the cart of volleyballs or stack of tumbling pads piled in the far corner. "You're new. You don't know how things are around here."

"Hailey's Queen of the Snobs, and those girls are vicious. You should just know what you're getting yourself into, that's all." Clare looked genuinely concerned.

"Well, I guess I've been warned. Thanks." Vivian hurried past their accusing stares and rushed toward the locker room. Heat flooded her cheeks as she hurried down the hall, tuning out the hushed whispers that followed her as she slipped through the rows of gym lockers. Classmates in various stages of undress stopped slipping off shoes and sports bras to gawk at her, as she blew past them.

She tugged her sweatshirt and jeans over her gym clothes and flung her backpack over one shoulder. As she dashed past the same girls she had passed coming in—still gawking, still removing sweaty gym shorts and tops—their stares followed her out. Clare, Emily, Tasha, and Gia were just entering the locker room as Vivian barreled through the door before it could swing shut behind them.

At least today was consistently crappy, Vivian thought as she walked briskly toward her locker to grab her jacket. *And at least it's finally over.*

CHAPTER SIX

TAKING THE STAIRS TWO AT A TIME, Vivian rushed to her room and slammed the door shut behind her. She was still angry about the girls at school making such a big deal over Grant being her partner in gym. They acted as if he wasn't allowed to talk to girls, just because he had a girlfriend. How stupid!

She opened her backpack and pulled out her history book. She had a lot of catching up to do, and maybe reading about the African slave trade would take her mind off how much she hated her new school.

She'd only been reading for twenty minutes when there was a knock at her door. She had blown past her father and Rebecca when she came home. The sound of them saying "hi" and asking how her day was followed her as she rushed toward her room. She figured her stomping up the stairs in a huff would put to rest any delusions that it had been anything other than utterly crappy.

"I'm studying!" she snapped.

Silence.

Good, she thought. *Maybe they'll just leave me alone the rest of the night. The last thing I want to do is deal with my dad and his wife trying to be my new best friends!*

She began to reread the paragraph she had been on before the interruption. Beyond the silence, she thought she heard something—the kind of sound that lingers on the corners of perception. It was almost inaudible. Or maybe it wasn't something she heard, but something she felt. It was as if someone were still outside her door. Waiting. Listening. Holding onto an inhaled breath while it whispered slowly through their lips.

She silently slid off her bed and tiptoed across the room. Crouching, she tilted her head and peered at the thin gap between the floor and the bottom of the door. Darkness broke the thin line of light that seeped through the crack as the shadow of someone—or something—swayed slightly.

She crept closer and pressed her ear to the door. Holding her breath, she listened. A light wheeze whispered against the mahogany. A shiver rippled through Vivian, as she pressed her ear firmly against the wooden panels. The air around her seemed to chill, raising the hairs on the back of her neck. She jumped back as a sharp knock splintered against the wood, causing her head to rattle from the vibration.

"Vivian? It's Anna."

"You scared the crap out of me!" Vivian laughed as she opened the door and motioned for her one and only new friend to come in. The coolness that had prickled her flesh seemed to rush out of the room, as Anna stepped across the threshold. Vivian quickly chalked the chill up to nerves.

"Sorry."

"No problem. Welcome to my bedroom! Don't ya love the décor?" She rolled her eyes in disgust as she plopped back onto her bed.

Anna laughed as she gazed at the mushroom-colored walls and sheer, flowing curtains. "It's kind of old fashioned, but it's pretty," she offered kindly. "It sounded like you wanted to be left alone, but I really wanted to ask you to go to the football game with me tonight."

Vivian crinkled her nose and gazed sadly at her history book. "I'm like seven chapters behind. I should probably stay home and study."

"I'm sure no one expects you to catch up in one day." Anna laughed and folded her hands in front as if she were praying. "Please, please, please!" she begged. "I really want to go, but I don't want to go alone. Tori and Zach are both in the pep band, so I can't sit with them, unless I steal a French horn from the band room. Please!"

"Okay, okay! Stop begging. I'll go." She slapped the hard, brown cover of her history book shut and slipped it into her backpack, before grabbing a sweatshirt out of her closet. "I'll have to clear it with the prison warden and his wife."

"I already talked to your dad, and he's cool with it. And Rebecca practically did a back flip when she heard me asking!"

They're probably thrilled that I've made a friend who actually wants to hang out with me. Like that will somehow make life normal, she thought, annoyed they might think she was acclimating to her environment. But looking at Anna, practically skipping down the hallway beside her, she did feel a sense of belonging that surprised her. She wasn't expecting to make a friend so quickly, but she was thankful she had.

Her father stood at the bottom of the stairs with her down vest, a stocking cap, and mittens laid out for her. It was as if he couldn't wait for her to leave.

"Nights get cold fast around here this time of year," he said, motioning toward the clothing on the step. "It's good to have a few layers on."

"Sure," Vivian mumbled as she slipped on her outerwear.

He rattled something in his pocket as he shifted his weight. Vivian raised an eyebrow at him, wondering why he looked so anxious.

"I won't be late," she offered, worried he might be having

second thoughts about letting her go out.

"Good," he smiled and seemed to relax a bit. His hand was still stuffed in his pocket, fidgeting with something that jingled quietly. "But if you want to stop out for a burger or something after the game, just call to let us know, so we don't worry. We'll be up."

"Okay."

"You have your cell phone, right?"

"Yes."

He pulled his jingling hand out of his pocket, revealing a set of car keys. "I thought you might like to drive yourself." He extended the keys to Vivian. "I pulled up a car out front that I thought might be fun for you girls to use."

Anna's eyes widened with excitement. Vivian held back her enthusiasm as she peered out the front window. A cherry-red, two-door, BMW was parked at the bottom of the porch steps.

"I hate to take your car, Dad. I mean it's really nice, but..." she wasn't sure what to say.

"I'd like you to try it out, Vivian. See what you think. If you like it, I thought it might be a good one for you to have. I'm sure you don't want to ride the bus to school every day."

Vivian resented the idea that he might be trying to buy her affections with an expensive car. But she also hated the idea of bouncing around on the green pleather seats of the school bus every day or depending on her dad and Rebecca for rides all the time.

Anna was practically jumping out of her shoes as she watched Vivian take the keys from her father and plod down the steps to what would probably become her new car.

Rebecca stood beside James on the porch, smiling and waving as if she'd just been crowned the new Miss USA. Her father didn't look quite so cheerful. The shadow on his shoulder had returned, only it had grown and taken the shape of a small person. Thin arms wrapped around James's neck, head cocked to one side near his ear, it crouched like a gargoyle upon his slumped shoulder.

For a moment, Vivian almost felt guilty as she watched the creature whispering into her father's ear through her rearview mirror. She knew her hate was feeding it—making it grow each time she glared at her father. She looked back to the road and tried to shake the image from her mind.

As they slowly rolled away from the circular drive toward the main lane leading to the highway, Vivian saw Raymond watching them from the barn. She waved at him as they passed. He did not return her wave. His face was etched with a look that could have been worry or anger, Vivian wasn't quite sure. There was no trace of a smile. He simply watched, stone-like from the massive doorway—silhouetted by bales of hay stacked nearly to the ceiling and cloaked by a black shadow figure which wrapped around his shoulders like a tar-colored cape.

Anna seemed completely unaware of him as they passed. She looked ahead beaming with excitement.

"Wow!" she exclaimed as they drove down the long lane, willows bowing toward them. "This sure beats my clunker!"

"I happen to like clunkers." Vivian smiled. "They're comfortable, like an old friend."

"New friends are nice too," Anna retorted. "And so are sweet cars!"

Both girls laughed as they turned onto the highway and headed toward the high school. Vivian was still a bit jumpy from the accident, so she kept the speedometer uncharacteristically under the posted speeds and slowed down cautiously as they met oncoming traffic. If Anna noticed her new friend's inclination to drive as if her passenger were a tester for the local DMV, she didn't say anything.

Easing off the gas, Vivian pulled into the farthest possible parking space, hoping to avoid being seen by too many of her new classmates. She did not want to deal with the condescending looks or the rude comments about her expensive car that they would whisper just loud enough for her to hear. Anna didn't question it as she leapt from the car and adjusted her stocking cap in the passenger side mirror.

Together, they hurried through the parking lot and into the stands. The cheerleaders were already on the track in front of the crowd, performing chants and getting the fans fired up with a few well-timed stunts.

"V-I-C-T-O-R-Y! That's our Bulldog battle cry!" Pompoms shook above their high ponytails and coordinated hair ribbons as they kicked their legs into the air. A crowd of young girls stood at the base of the stands, chanting along as they clapped their hands to the rhythm.

The drum major stood before several stands filled with instrument-holding students. She clapped twice before raising her arms above her head. Her fingers outstretched as if she might be trying to use "the Force" on the obedient pep band that simultaneously raised their instruments to their mouths. Trumpets and horns blasted out a song, causing the crowd to rise to their feet.

The cheerleaders twirled and shook in synchronized motions as the young pack of future high-school cheerleaders standing in the crowd before them copied each move.

"All hail, Richfield High School. We're here one hundred million strong..." The crowd, young and old, belted out the words to the school song.

Small town school pride is pretty impressive, Vivian thought. *I guess that's one thing they have over my old school. I'm pretty sure that's the only thing.*

Vivian watched the football team rush the field. She quickly zoned in on Grant. His white football pants hugged his thighs like bark on a tree, pressed tightly against each ripple of muscle that tensed and flexed as he bounded across the field.

Okay, maybe it's not the only thing, she mused with a grin.

As the team spread out along the sidelines, she noticed Grant squinting into the stands, his helmet sandwiched between his bicep and chest. His eyes settled on a section a few feet away from Vivian, and he waved.

A woman, wrapped in a red and black Bulldog's blanket waved back. She wore a black baseball cap pulled low over her forehead and a button on her chest with a picture of Grant in his jersey, holding a football.

As he began to turn his head to face his teammates, Grant locked eyes with Vivian. The knit hat her father had given her hugged her head tightly as she rubbed her mittened hands together, trying to warm them with friction. Grant's smile widened as his hand waved above his head.

It seemed like he was looking at her, but Vivian looked around to make sure no one else was waving back before returning his smile. She wasn't quite brave enough to return the wave, still afraid it was intended for some other chilled, pep-filled fan.

Seeing her unsure smile, Grant slipped his helmet onto his head, tossed an invisible ball into the air and swatted at it, as if serving it across a net. When Vivian laughed and finally waved, he turned his back to the crowd and joined his huddled teammates.

Vivian could not hide her happiness at Grant's greeting.

"Be careful, girl." Anna smiled coyly as she raised an eyebrow at Vivian's sudden smile. "He's got a girlfriend, and she's not what you'd call friendly."

Both girl's glanced down at the track and watched as the cheerleaders launched Grant's pretty girlfriend into a high basket-toss. Hailey touched her toes at the peak of her ascent, and flashed a wide-mouthed smile before landing in a snare of arms.

Vivian rolled her eyes and breathed out heavily. "So I've heard. Anyway, I'm pretty sure I'm not competition for his perfect ten."

"She's far from perfect," Anna replied. "But don't tell her that! She'd never believe you!"

Somewhere between kickoff and second quarter, Vivian realized she should have grabbed something to eat at home before rushing out the door. The sound of her growling stomach was muffled by the cheers of the fans, as Grant threw a pass into the end zone. Number twenty-three snared the spiraling ball in a cradle catch, raising the scoreboard numbers in their favor: twenty-one to seven.

"I'm starving," she shouted over the roar of fans. "I'm gonna hit the concession stand. Do you want anything?"

"No thanks. I'm good." Anna's reply barely carried over the rumbling cheers of the fans.

As the offense lined up for the extra-point kick, Vivian worked her way through the crowd. She passed the woman Grant had waved at earlier. Vivian assumed she must be his mother.

She smiled sheepishly at Vivian as they crossed paths. Though the baseball cap was pulled low over her forehead, Vivian could see her right eye bore the gray-blue hues of a bruise. Vivian returned the woman's smile and quickly looked away, suddenly afraid she might appear to be staring at the blackened eye.

As Vivian neared the end of the bleachers, she glanced back at the woman. A small shadow covered her like a backpack. A black tail, longer than the rest of its body, wagged behind it like a happy puppy. Clawed fingers dug into her rounded shoulders. Vivian felt a pang of sadness for the woman as she and her dark passenger were swallowed by the crowd.

Vivian wandered around the side of the building behind the stands. The restrooms sat silently along the dark side of the building. The sound of hungry fans making their food selection at the concession stand around the corner was barely audible over the thunder of feet stomping a rhythm against the metal bleachers as the crowd chanted, "Defense!"

Vivian decided she'd slip into the restroom before getting a hotdog from the concession stand. The metal door of the lady's room groaned in protest as she pushed. Before it could fully open, the hinges stuck, forcing Vivian to press her weight into her shoulder and heave. The chill of cold steel cut through her sweatshirt as the door was thrust into the dimly lit chamber. A single light hung from the center of the small, concrete room housing two teal-green toilet stalls. The dull, yellow glow made the room feel hazy and left the corners of the walls darker than the night outside.

A thin girl in a cheerleading sweater and pleated skirt stood near the far corner staring sadly at her reflection in the hazy mirror above a sink. The hollow, steady dripping of water echoed off the basin in front of her. She sniffled quietly and wiped at a tear as it rolled down her cheek.

"Hey." Vivian smiled sympathetically. She felt the urge to join her in front of the mirror and cry with her. Lately, she had found a good, hard cry could almost make her feel better, if only for a moment. Letting her sadness pour out somehow made her feel alive again. For a few tear-drenched moments, she felt something—which was somehow better than the deep, dark emptiness that made her heart pulse with loneliness and grief.

"Are you okay?"

The girl drew a sharp breath, as if startled by Vivian's voice. Vivian thought it was strange the girl hadn't heard her body-slam the door open, just a few moments earlier. But she knew all too well how easy it was to sometimes become completely lost in your own sadness.

"I don't mean to be nosy," Vivian offered. "I just noticed you're crying. Is there anything I can do?"

The girl gazed at Vivian, and her mouth parted slightly as if she wanted to say something but couldn't quite find the words. She looked down at the gray concrete floor and shook her head. Straight blond hair swayed loosely around her pale cheeks.

"No." Her voice was as thin as a trickle of water. Although Vivian had to strain to hear the word, she had the strange sense that it had been whispered directly into her ear. A shiver ran through her. She took a few steps back, feeling a sudden urge to turn and leave.

Stop being so stupid, she scolded herself. *For cripes sake, just go to the bathroom!*

Slipping quietly into the stall closest to the door, Vivian slid the lock into place. She listened as the strange girl cried quietly. As Vivian flushed the toilet and snapped her jeans, the bathroom door moaned open. Heavy footsteps rushed across the bare concrete. Vivian's hand was just about to slide the lock open, when she heard the girl.

"Please don't," she whimpered.

Vivian stepped back from the stall door, unsure of what to do. Terror had frozen her where she stood. The stillness of the room was broken by a sudden slash of metal against air. The stirred breeze was pierced by a scream that ricocheted off the concrete walls. Vivian could hear the fast movement of a struggle beyond the teal frame around her. She moved further into the corner of the stall and breathlessly tried to hide behind the ceramic bowl of the toilet.

Heavy footsteps hurried toward the exit. The door seemed to shriek at the assailant as it was pulled open and slammed shut, sealing the bathroom like a tomb.

The seconds Vivian stood shaking in the corner of the stall seemed to hang endlessly in time. Air she had held in her lungs spilled past her lips in jagged, quivering breaths. With trembling fingers, she fumbled with the sliding lock and stepped cautiously out of her hiding place. She was almost certain the attacker had left, but she was gripped by the fear that they could have pretended to leave and might be waiting just inside the door, like a wolf lying in wait for a frightened rabbit to peek from its hiding place.

She glanced first toward the door, and saw that no one was there. Slowly, she turned her gaze toward the sink where the girl had been standing and braced her mind for the horror she was certain she was about to see.

The faucet dripped a slow rhythm as Vivian's throat tightened, and her head began to spin. Her eyes widened as her mouth dropped open.

There was no one there.

The room was cold and empty. So cold, in fact, that her breath puffed a chilled cloud in front of her as she gasped in surprise. Rubbing a finger across her throbbing scar, she backed toward the exit.

The piercing howl of hinges made Vivian spin around. Anna, stood cautiously just beyond the threshold.

"What are you doing in here?" she peered cautiously past Vivian into the bathroom. She stayed just outside. "Get out of there!"

"What? Why?" Vivian stammered as she staggered toward Anna, her legs weak and trembling as she glanced over her shoulder toward the sink.

A hazy outline of the girl stood in front of the mirror. She turned toward Vivian, fading in and out of visibility, flickering like an old projector clicking over slides. For a second, Vivian and the girl made eye contact.

"How can you see me?" she whispered. "I'm dead."

Anna grabbed Vivian's hand and pulled her out of the restroom. The door slammed behind them. A padlock dangled from a heavy chain, swaying like a noose from the metal handle.

Vivian gasped as cold air filled her lungs. She leaned against Anna, trying to steady herself as her knees threatened to buckle beneath her.

"How'd you even get in there?" Anna glanced at the padlock dangling from the door.

Vivian followed her gaze. "It was unlocked," she stammered. "I had to go to the bathroom, so I went in." She squinted at the chain that still rattled against the metal door. "I didn't even notice that was on there."

"I can't believe it was unlocked," Anna said staring at the rusted metal lock. "No one's been in there for over a year. Not since Nancy Taylor..." Her voice trailed off.

"She was murdered," Vivian said as she stared at the shut door, happy to be on the other side of it.

"Yeah. How'd you know?"

"I just...well, you acted like you didn't want to step foot in there. So I figured it must have been something really bad."

"Yeah. It was awful. They say she was stabbed like fifty times..." Anna gazed solemnly toward the closed door. "They still don't know who did it!"

"That's horrible!" Vivian could hear the thin whisper of Nancy replay in her head. *"I'm dead..."*

As Vivian glanced toward the closed door, a sliver of darkness rose almost imperceptibly behind Anna, as if it had slipped under the base of the door. A flash of pain above her brow caused Vivian to wince. She closed her eyes against the throbbing that had migrated from her scar into the back of her head.

She hadn't been prone to headaches before the accident, but they seemed to strike her now any time she became stressed. The doctor thought, over time, she would have them less often. She hoped he was right.

"Are you okay?" Anna asked as Vivian grasped her arm and peeked at her through squinted eyes. The shadow Vivian thought she had seen was gone.

"My head...hurts..." she said, her teeth grinding as the throbbing intensified.

"Maybe I should call your dad," Anna suggested, her voice tight with concern.

"No. Really, I'll be okay. Maybe you could just drive me

home." Her voice sounded more pathetic than she had hoped, as she grasped her head in her hands. "It's just my stupid head injury from the accident. Sometimes it hurts really badly. I'm sorry to make you miss the game."

"Don't worry about it. If you've seen Grant Jackson win one game, you've seen them all!" She tried to sound cheerful as she supported the weight of her new friend and led her away from the doomed bathroom toward the parking lot. "Besides, this means I get to drive your car. And I'm totally going to use this whole 'my friend's sick' thing as an excuse to drive crazy fast!"

Vivian smiled through her pain. "You have my permission to go as fast as you want." Vivian felt as if she were walking through a haze that threatened to swallow her. With each step, she felt as if she were stepping deeper and deeper into darkness. Fear tightened her throat.

Her mind replayed the events in the bathroom as Anna drove her home, staying true to her promise to drive fast.

She wanted to ask Anna about the girl who was murdered, but the combination of her throbbing head and Anna's erratic driving had Vivian breathing deeply, trying not to vomit on the leather seats of her new car.

"You don't look so good," Thane whispered into her ear.

She peered through the corner of her eye to see him leaning up from the back seat.

"Where have you been?" she asked, still trying to breathe back the bile rising in her throat. *"I could have used you about an hour ago, to warn me there was a dead girl in the bathroom!"*

"I'm sorry. I wish I could be with you all the time, but you know it doesn't work that way."

"What's the use of having a brother on the 'other-side' if he can't keep me from stumbling into dead chicks?"

"Was she cute?"

Vivian tried not to laugh out loud as she peered out the window. *"Actually, yeah! Do you want me to get her number the next time I run into her?"*

Thane laughed. *"Nah. I'm too busy for girls right now."*

The throbbing in her head began to ease as she relaxed in the comfort of her brother's presence. Anna turned the corner like a get-away-car driver in a bad cop movie, and then eased up on the gas as they traveled the long, tree-shrouded driveway leading to Vivian's house.

"How are you feeling over there?"

"A little better, now that the trees aren't flying past my window at a hundred miles an hour," Vivian teased.

"I wasn't going that fast. I never got over ninety-five, I swear!" she joked back. "Seriously, I hope my driving didn't make you sick. You turned a couple shades of green back there. I was kind of expecting you to throw up!"

"So was I!" Vivian opened her door. The cool September breeze sent a shiver through her.

"That would have been sweet!" Thane interjected enthusiastically.

"Do you want me to walk you in?" Anna offered as she stepped out of the car and gazed back at Vivian.

"No, thanks." Vivian smiled more cheerfully than she truly felt. "I'm okay." A gust of wind blew her voice across the driveway, chasing after a clump of leaves that scattered noisily. "Sorry I ruined your night."

"You didn't." Anna smiled, her eyes sparkling in the moonlight.

Anna rounded the car and headed up the driveway towards the far side of the house. She turned and waved a hand. "Night, Viv," she called out.

"See ya!" Vivian waved back. As Anna disappeared into the darkness, Vivian thought she heard a twig snap in the opposite direction. Squinting, she peered into the dimly-lit yard. The pale light of the lampposts cast long, scattered shadows across the grass. Vivian quivered in the chilled air, as she slowly backed toward the porch steps, still scanning the murkiness surrounding her.

A cat darted out of the darkness across the driveway. Vivian relaxed as she blew a heavy breath.

Scared by a stupid cat, she thought as she peered around, looking for Thane. Once again, he'd vanished as quickly as he had appeared. Disappointed he was already gone, she bounded up the steps, and slipped quietly through the front door.

Her father was sitting on the sofa near the fireplace in the room just off the foyer. He glanced up at her, as he laid his opened book face down on the arm of the sofa.

"Home so soon?" he asked warmly.

"I had a headache."

As he rose and walked toward her, furrowing his brow in worry, she backed toward the steps.

"It's not so bad now, though," she assured him.

"Do you need anything? I have your pills in the kitchen, if you need one."

Her scar still throbbed as if a tiny creature was inside of it, trying to pound its way through her flesh.

"Maybe I should have one."

She hated the pills the doctor had prescribed her. They made her feel disconnected from herself, almost as if she had no control over her own body. But she had to admit, her head never hurt after she took one.

Within a few minutes, her father was back from the kitchen with a pill and a glass of cool water. She placed the capsule on her tongue and quickly chugged the water down. After putting the empty glass into her father's outstretched hand, she turned her back to him and headed toward the staircase.

"Thanks," she mumbled, before quickly ascended the steps.

"Vivian," her father said.

She stopped a few steps from the top and slowly looked

over her shoulder. "What?" she asked quietly.

He bit his lip and looked at his feet. The small demon on his shoulder seemed to grow before Vivian's eyes. She looked away, not wanting to face the darkness she knew she was creating around him with her anger.

"Just let me know if you need anything." He smiled uncomfortably. "Goodnight."

"Night," she said, rounding the corner of the landing and rushing to her room. As she opened her bedroom door, she peered down the long, dark hallway toward the room at the top of the stairs. The door was closed, and all was quiet—for now.

The pill her father had given her was already starting to take effect, by the time she had slipped into her sweatpants and Thane's old Yankee's shirt. Her head began to feel like a balloon filled with helium.

She laid her head on her pillow and closed her eyes. Her body felt as if it would float off the bed, if it were not held down by her comforter. She was half-asleep as her medication took full control of her body.

As she flitted between consciousness and unconsciousness, she began to dream that she was a young girl—about four years old. Her mother pushed Vivian on a swing, her hair flowing in the breeze as she giggled. Her father pushed Thane on a swing beside her. The gentle melody of his laughter floated through her ears.

Somewhere behind the joyful sounds, Vivian heard a voice that made her heart race.

"I'm watching you," it hissed.

She felt hot breath on her cheek as her mind raced out of her dream and back into her body which lay rooted to her bed. Her eyelids were like lead as she struggled to open them. She managed to pry them open for a second—a blur of a face with hollowed eye sockets stared back at her. Hot breath huffed against her cheeks. The warmth was quickly replaced by a sudden chill caused by the frigid air against her flesh, which had been moistened by the sulfurous exhalation against it. The stench of rot filled her nostrils like old garbage left in the sun to fester.

Her eyes slammed shut against her will, as she fought to keep them open. Raising her eyebrows, she struggled against the weight of her drug-induced drowsiness. The sound of staggered breaths, like those of a bird dog searching out a pheasant in a field of tall grass, filled the space around Vivian's incapacitated body. She felt as if she were awake, yet in a nightmare.

As her eyes fluttered open, the smell vanished. The warmth of the hot, damp breath on her cheek was gone. Her room was black and empty. And silent. Her eyelids were like slabs of concrete as they slammed shut.

There's nothing there. It's just that stupid medicine making me imagine things, she reasoned, as her mind wandered uneasily back into her dream where she was once again young and happy.

She and Thane slid down the slide together, their parents waiting for them at the bottom. Across the green grass of the playground, beyond rows of daisies and poppies, stood a pretty girl with long, blond hair. She seemed to be watching Vivian and her family. Her short, red, pleated skirt billowed gently, as a breeze scattered flower petals through the air.

The girl flashed a pretty smile and waved. Vivian waved back and ran through the grass toward her.

"Nancy, come play with us," she called across the rows of flowers.

"I can't," Nancy replied sadly, all of the happiness drained from her face.

As Vivian got closer, she saw that another girl sat at Nancy's feet. Her head buried in her hands as silent sobs shook her shoulders. Around Nancy's wrist was a thin metal chain which trailed down toward the other girl. The other end of the chain was fastened to the crying girl's wrist. Tears dripped from the smooth, metal links, as they spilled from the covered eyes of the girl. Her brown, shoulder-length hair shrouded her face.

"Help us, please." Nancy's voice was caught with a gust of wind that pushed Vivian back toward the playground, where her family stood watching her. She seemed to be as light as a slip of paper. In a moment, the two girls were tiny silhouettes—so far away that Vivian would not have known they were girls at all, if she had not just been standing in front of them.

"Help us, Vivian," Nancy's voice called across the breeze. "Please, help us."

CHAPTER SEVEN

VIVIAN FOUND HER STEPMOTHER READING A magazine at the kitchen table the next morning. Rebecca's hair was pulled back into such a tiny ponytail it resembled the stub of a cropped dog tail. Bobby pins held the lose strands, too short to reach the elastic holder, off of her face. That hairstyle would have looked ridiculous on most women, but it seemed to highlight Rebecca's high cheekbones even more than usual.

"Good morning," she said, as she set the magazine on the table "Your dad is already off at a business meeting. He said you came home with quite a headache last night. Are you feeling better?"

"Yes. Just a little groggy."

"Pain medication can have that effect on a person. Nothing a cup of coffee can't fix." She smiled as she filled a cup from the carafe in the center of the table and pushed the steaming mug toward an open seat beside her.

"How was the game?"

"I only got to see part of it, before I got sick." Vivian stirred the cream into her coffee before taking a sip, wondering if she should ask her stepmother about what was really on her mind. After a long pause, she cleared her throat nervously and said, "Anna told me about a girl who was murdered at the school last year."

"I heard about that. It's so sad," Rebecca said, looking at Vivian cautiously.

"It's okay. I can handle talking about sad stuff," Vivian said, sensing Rebecca's hesitation. "I'm not as fragile as you guys think."

Rebecca nodded. "I was hoping you could get a bit more settled before you started hearing about all that, but I suppose it's inevitable."

"What do you know about it?"

"Not much." Rebecca shrugged. "I know a girl your age named Nancy was murdered last year at the school. Most people thought it was a stranger—someone passing through town. No one wants to think there's a murderer living among them. But then Sarah Christian went missing, and people began to wonder if the two cases were related."

"Another girl my age?"

"Yes." Rebecca shifted uncomfortably in her seat. She looked at Vivian as if she wanted to say something but wasn't sure how to phrase it.

"What?" Vivian asked.

Rebecca bit her lip and looked around the room, before taking a sip of her coffee.

"Whatever it is, I can handle it," Vivian said as she began to feel nervous, wondering what Rebecca might be so hesitant to tell her.

"Sarah's family owned this home before us. She lived here when she disappeared."

The shrill of the telephone ringing made both Vivian and Rebecca jump. She looked at Vivian sympathetically, before rising from the table to answer it.

"Hello," Rebecca said. The rosy pink of her cheeks seemed to drain from her face. "Is he ok? I'll be right there!"

She placed the receiver into the cradle before turning to Vivian. "Your father's been admitted to the hospital. He was having chest pains. The doctor is fairly certain it was a severe anxiety attack, but they're running some tests now to be sure."

"Oh, no!" Vivian said. A worried knot immediately tightened her stomach.

"I'm sure he's fine. He's been under so much stress lately. This isn't the first time he's had an anxiety attack, but you really can't be too careful at his age." Rebecca eased Vivian's worry with a smile. "Don't tell him I referred to him as being old enough to be on heart attack alert. I should go to him, though!" Rebecca grabbed her purse and keys off the counter near the back door.

Vivian wondered how much of her father's stress had been created by her presence. "Of course! I'll be fine here," she said.

"Are you sure?"

"Yes. Go."

"I'll call as soon as I know anything." Rebecca hurried through the kitchen.

Please let him be alright. Vivian was a little surprised to hear her own thoughts, but a delinquent parent was probably better than being an orphan, she reasoned.

Vivian heard the front door shut behind Rebecca, leaving her alone in the house she just learned had been the home of a girl who vanished. Well, almost alone. A chill ran up Vivian's spine. Beyond the silence of the empty rooms, somewhere past the gentle tick of the grandfather clock in the sitting room, just behind the light rush of leaves against the porch that circled the house, something stirred. She felt it more than she heard it. But she knew it was there.

Then she saw it. An apparition not fully formed, but solid enough for Vivian to recognize as the shape of a girl. Her blurred and colorless features formed a wispy silhouette of white.

A puddle of coffee formed around Vivian's mug as she set it on the table with trembling hands. The figure floated through the kitchen and into the long hallway leading to the front entry of the home. Without hesitation, Vivian rose to follow it, walking on her tiptoes as if the sound of her footsteps might startle the apparition and cause it to disappear.

Even in the daylight, the hallway was shrouded in darkness, nearly void of any natural light. As the wispy form reached the closed door in the center of the hallway, it paused, turned to face Vivian, and pointed at the door before flickering and fading into the shadows of the corridor.

Vivian quickened her steps to stand in the same spot the apparition had been just seconds before. As she opened the closed door, she stood above a long, narrow stairwell that seemed to disappear into a black hole. Running her hand along the walls inside the door, Vivian flipped a light switch. A bare bulb hung in the ceiling at the bottom of the steps, casting an unnaturally dull, yellow glow around the space below.

Vivian shuddered as she began to move cautiously down the steps. The boards beneath her feet had grayed with age and bore a worn trail where a century of footsteps had gone before her. With each descent, the temperature of the air around her seemed to drop, causing gooseflesh to spike on her arms. She rubbed at them as she crossed her arms in front of herself in an attempt to contain her own body heat, suddenly aware of how thin the t-shirt was that she had worn to bed.

With a final step down, the startling chill of the concrete against her bare feet sent a shiver through her body. Vivian squinted into the darkness. A single, bare bulb dangled loosely on an extension cord strung across the thick ceiling beams—an afterthought to a basement once lit only by candles and kerosene lamps. The hazy glow was quickly swallowed by the corners of the immense space.

Across the room, somewhere in the shadows, Vivian saw the wisp of white reappear. The featureless shape of a girl flickered just long enough for Vivian to see her point toward the wall in the farthest corner of the basement, before fading away into the darkness.

Almost against her will, Vivian's feet moved steadily across the cold, cracked concrete, layered in decades of dust. As her eyes adjusted to the darkness, she saw that the shadows along the plaster walls moved slowly, slithering from the floor to the ceiling. Undead, but not quite alive, they morphed into shapes resembling creatures, before slipping flat against the walls again. They seemed to watch Vivian as she cautiously reached out to touch the wall.

Running her fingers along the crumbling plaster, Vivian walked slowly, deliberately searching with each step. For what, she wasn't sure, but she was compelled to search. When she found it, whatever it was, she was certain she would know.

Plaster flaked away at her touch, and then the texture beneath her fingertips changed to the porous chill of brick. Vivian leaned in until the red-fired stone was visible just inches from her face. It seemed to be much newer than the surrounding walls, untouched by the years that had cracked and peeled the finish from the plaster.

Each brick was firmly pressed against the next, then her hand felt one brick move as she touched it. Air lightly whistled through the loose bricks, as if someone—or something – stood on the other side blowing. Vivian pressed a little harder until she felt the brick completely give away. A rush of stale air shot from the hole, blowing Vivian's hair away from her face. The light bulb swayed in the breeze.

Compelled by a force beyond her understanding, Vivian attacked the wall, pulling and pushing one brick after another away from the barrier between her and something. What, she wasn't sure, but she was certain that the spirit who had led her here needed her to see beyond this wall. The dust created by the flurry of falling bricks made a cloudy haze envelop the already dark room. The sound of the bricks thudding against the concrete floor was so deafening, Vivian barely heard the stairs creak behind her.

She froze, her heart thudding against her chest, a brick she had just shimmied out of the wall clenched in her hands. She turned around, peering through the plume of dust that seemed to swirl around the air as if it were being stirred like a creamy soup of grime and grit. The air was like fog on a steamy night, leaving her able to see only a few inches in front of her face. The stairs were hidden in the churning haze.

Vivian held her breath as she listened to the silence. The light swayed loosely above the room, making the cloud of dust particles even more disorienting.

Maybe I imagined the creak. Maybe it was just a bit of a brick that broke off and scattered when I dropped it to the ground. Maybe I'm just...

Creak. Then a footstep descended on the wooden steps. Then another. Slowly. Frighteningly slow. As if the person was contemplating what they would actually do when they got to the final step. The bulb swayed slightly and then went black.

Like a panicked rabbit rushing into a burrow away from its prey, Vivian squeezed through the hole she had created in the wall. Somehow, the darkness of the basement behind her became even darker. Her hands flailed in front of and around her, her sense of sight totally useless to her in the pitch black consuming her.

The cold and cracked concrete floor gave way to the cool smoothness of packed earth. The smell of dirt filled her nostrils as her breaths came jagged and panicked into her lungs. She moved slightly to her right, her hands outstretched, until she felt the chill of the wall beneath her palms. Using the wall to balance and guide herself in the disorienting darkness, she rushed forward, deeper into darkness, farther away from the basement behind her. The echoes of her own staggered breaths startled her. The sound of breathing seemed to be all around her, and if someone else's breaths were mingled with her own, she feared she would not know the difference.

Cautiously, Vivian peered back as she stumbled forward. And then, a dull light sprung on in the basement behind her, revealing the cramped tunnel she was moving through. No wider than four feet, no taller than seven feet. She had managed to put about twenty yards between herself and the hole she had shimmied through. She continued to move forward as she watched behind her. The thought that someone might crawl through the hole almost crippled her with fear, but her feet stumbled forward. She had put another ten yards between herself and the hole, when the shadow of a body covered the hole and blocked out the dull light seeping through it.

Fueled by terror, Vivian broke into a full sprint.

CHAPTER EIGHT

VIVIAN RAN UNTIL HER OUTSTRETCHED ARMS slammed into something solid. The wind momentarily knocked out of her, her hands frantically searched the wooden plank in front of her. When she felt the cool knob against her palm, she grabbed and twisted. Pulling, then pushing, the door jiggled, but would not budge. She turned the knob frantically again, tears streaming down her cheeks, and slammed her body into the door before it moved forward.

She spilled into a small room and careened toward a set of wooden, plank steps, similar to those in the basement at the other end of the tunnel. Above the steps, light peeked through the knotty holes and splits in the planks of a wooden door in the ceiling. Vivian rushed up the steps and used her shoulder to heave the door upward. Sunlight shocked her eyes, making her squeeze them shut, as she stepped onto the floorboards of a small room, before letting the door beneath her slam shut. She realized that she was in the coal shed in the woodland behind her house.

Fearful that whoever had entered the basement in the house might have followed her, she rushed toward a door with a single window framed in the center. Years of dirt gave the window a tinted quality, but the stark change from blackness to light was still painful to Vivian's eyes. She sprinted from the small building into the sunlight penetrating through the clearing in the trees around her.

She ran until she was deep into the forest, before dropping to her knees behind a large pine tree to catch her breath. Peering back, she could see the small shed partially hidden by trees and brush. Everything around her was still. Almost unnaturally still. There were no sounds of birds or bugs or forest critters scurrying about—just dead silence. Until the front door of the shed slammed shut.

Vivian sprang from her hiding place and raced through the woods toward the house. A string of questions played through her mind.

What if whoever came into the basement catches me? What if it wasn't them at all? Maybe it was just the wind catching the door. Maybe it hadn't shut all the way, after I ran out. What if they're still in the house?

She slowed her sprint to a jog, looking over her shoulder every few steps.

What should I do? If I go back to the house, they may still be there.

She turned her course slightly and headed toward the small cabin she had noticed down the road from the barn. She jogged briskly through the trees, twigs and dried leaves crunching beneath her bare feet. A rabbit scurried from behind a bush and disappeared behind another. A bird chirped a sudden song somewhere above her. And just like that, the forest seemed to come back to life. Vivian came to the gravel road leading to Raymond and Anna's small house. When she saw Anna sitting on the porch swing, a book in her hand, Vivian broke into a run again until she plodded up the fronts steps of the porch. The scratches on her feet burned as sweat dripped down her legs.

Anna looked up from her book, startled by the sudden intrusion.

"Where did you come from?" she asked. "You look like you just saw a ghost or something. What's wrong?"

"My dad is in the hospital," Vivian stammered through short breaths. "Rebecca had to go be with him..."

"Oh no! Is he okay?"

"No...I mean...yes." Vivian struggled to keep her thoughts straight. "I mean, I think so. They think he had an anxiety attack."

"Oh, thank goodness!"

"But I was alone in the house, and I went to the basement and someone came after me down there!"

Anna jumped up from the swing. "Who? What do you mean, they came after you?"

"I don't know who. They shut the light off on me down there, and I ran through the tunnel!"

"The tunnel? But that's been sealed up since your dad and Rebecca moved in."

"Rebecca told me about Sarah Christian this morning." Vivian slowly sank onto the swing, suddenly too exhausted to stand.

"She did? What'd she tell you?"

"Just that she had lived here when she went missing. That's why I went down there...I think...I don't know really."

"You're not making much sense, Vivian. You're kind of scaring me," Anna said, settling onto the swing beside her.

"I'm sorry." Vivian buried her head into her hands. "I'm scaring myself. I don't know what's going on anymore."

Dust billowed from the driveway near the main house, as a red truck turned onto the side road and pulled into the barn.

"Look, my dad's back from town. Let's go have him help us figure out what's going on." Anna pulled Vivian up from the swing by her elbow and pushed a pair of flip flops from the rug by the door in front of Vivian's feet.

"Throw these on," Anna said as she led Vivian down the steps. Together, they jogged the half-mile to the barn and stopped inside the opened door.

Anna quickly told him what Vivian said had happened in the basement. Raymond looked skeptical. Or maybe he was worried. Vivian wasn't sure. He was difficult to read. But he grabbed a tire iron from the back of the truck before jogging toward the back porch on the main house.

Vivian and Anna stood outside, watching the door after it shut behind him. They waited for what felt like forever, but in reality had only been about ten minutes. The door opened, and Raymond emerged, followed by a petite woman whose hair was pulled high in a ponytail. She wore jeans and a sweatshirt and carried a caddy of cleaning supplies in one hand.

"Marybeth," Anna breathed the name with relief. She looked at Vivian and smiled. "She's the housekeeper."

Vivian looked from Anna to the woman, then back to Anna.

"I am so sorry! When I saw the basement door open and the light on down there, I just figured Ms. Rebecca had forgotten to shut it off. We passed her in the driveway as she left. I'm afraid I forgot you might be home." The woman bit her lower lip and looked down at her feet. "I'm so terribly sorry."

Raymond patted the woman gently on the back, "You didn't mean anything by it, Marybeth. Ms. Vivian is okay, aren't ya, ma'am?"

Vivian was struck by the woman's hunched shoulders and the small, black shadow perched upon them. She looked like a dog that was afraid to be kicked. Then the woman raised her head slightly to look at Vivian. A blue-gray bruise circled her right eye. Without the baseball cap, Vivian hadn't recognized her at first, but as their eyes connected, she knew immediately that Marybeth was the woman she had assumed was Grant's mom at the game the night before.

"Oh, I'm fine." Vivian said. "I was just startled, really."

"I feel terrible. Raymond said you ran through the tunnel to the coal shed. You must have been terrified." Marybeth looked toward the ground again.

"I probably needed a good jog, anyway." Vivian smiled, as Marybeth raised her head again.

"No harm done, Marybeth," Raymond assured her. He patted her shoulder again, almost fatherly.

"I'll get back to my work, then," she said sheepishly.

"Mind if I borrow that young man of yours to unload the grain bags from the truck?" Raymond asked.

"Not at all," Marybeth replied. "He's on the front porch studying."

"He's a good boy," Raymond said. "Just like his mother."

Marybeth blushed before turning to go into the house. "He is a good boy," she replied before entering the back door.

Raymond walked around the porch and paused when he got to Vivian and Anna. "Are you sure you're okay, Ms. Vivian?" He looked at her with concern etched across the lines of his forehead.

"I'm alright," she assured him.

He continued around the porch before slipping out of sight. Anna looked at Vivian closely.

"But didn't you think someone was down there?" Anna asked.

"I thought someone was, but it was dusty, and I couldn't see well." Anna eyed her with a bit of skepticism. "Anyway, my doctor warned me about post-traumatic stress. He said it may make me more jumpy than usual."

"I suppose crawling through a wall might qualify as jumpy."

Vivian's mind raced behind the smile she gave her friend. Something was down there—she was sure of it. But she wasn't about to wave her freak flag and tell her one and only new friend that a ghost had led her to the basement. And she sure wasn't going to say that she was convinced that there was an evil spirit living inside the house, or that she thought it may have followed her into the basement.

Anna raised an eyebrow and nodded toward the barn. "Wanna watch Grant Jackson flex his pipes and get sweaty while he helps my dad unload seeds?"

"Don't mind if I do," Vivian replied, happy to have a distraction from the worry twisting her stomach into knots. Instead of thinking about the missing girl who used to live in her house, or the ghost girl who she assumed might be the same girl, or the creepy shadow creature living in the bedroom at the top of the stairs, who may have just chased Vivian through a dark tunnel in the basement, Vivian sat beside her friend on the side porch facing the barn, their feet kicked up on the railing as they watched Grant, his shirt thrown on the hood of the truck, his muscles glistening with sweat, as he lifted one bag of grain after another out of the truck bed.

CHAPTER NINE

VIVIAN SAT ON THE PORCH SWING watching the sun sink behind the row of willows along the driveway. Her stepmother had called an hour ago, saying they were leaving the hospital soon. Marybeth and Grant left just after Rebecca called, after Marybeth put a stew to simmer on the stove for dinner and apologized to Vivian for the millionth time.

As they left, she noticed how attentive Grant was to his mother. He had insisted on carrying her supplies to the car for her. He had even opened the passenger door and helped her into the seat before getting behind the wheel himself to drive them away. He seemed protective and almost paternal in the way he cared for her. Vivian sensed from Marybeth's demeanor and the bruise on her eye that she might have been a victim of domestic violence. She wondered if Grant was trying to compensate for the love his mother lacked from an abusive husband, and she began to understand why the boy who seemed to have it all might sometimes have a demon on his back.

Grant had kept busy helping Raymond with chores around the barn. Vivian and Anna unabashedly took in the view for a while, as they sat on the porch together. Grant waved once and smiled at Vivian more times than she could count. Every time he looked at her, she wondered if her face looked as hot as it felt. She was certain her cheeks were about to burst into flames whenever she noticed him glancing her way, which, according to Anna, was four-hundred and twenty-three times, give or take a glance or two.

Before Anna had gone back to her house, Vivian made Anna run up to her bedroom with her to grab her history book, so she could try to catch up. She felt foolish that she was too nervous to be in the house, especially since everyone had easily explained away the incident that had sent her stumbling through a bricked-up, pitch-black, underground tunnel, but if Anna found her fear silly, she didn't let on to it. Anna chattered from the porch, through the house, up the staircase, and back down again, where Vivian settled onto the porch swing. Vivian found her new friend to be an unexpected source of comfort. Anna's gossip about the kids at school, most of whom Vivian didn't know yet, calmed her worry and made her feel like just another teen in Richfield, if only for the moment.

Vivian thought she should go inside to stir the stew again, but that would mean walking past the basement door, and she wasn't ready for that quite yet, at least not when no one else was home. She had spent the last forty-five minutes with her history book opened to the first page of chapter two, replaying the events in the basement.

She almost had herself convinced that she had overreacted to Marybeth turning the light off. The footsteps coming down the steps could have just been Marybeth stepping briefly onto the stairs to find the light switch. Maybe the light had not come back on, and the hole in the wall had not been covered by the form of someone looking in after her. Maybe the post-traumatic stress her doctor had warned her about was causing her to find terror where there was none.

But the girl had led her there—that she was certain of. Although her spirit had only flickered before her for a moment, she was also quite sure it was Sarah Christian's spirit trying to tell her something. Which meant the girl who had lived in this house before her wasn't just missing—she was dead.

The thought frightened her. She wished Thane would make an appearance. She worried he would eventually leave altogether. She knew it was selfish to want his spirit to remain in limbo, somewhere between eternity and her own present, but she couldn't stop hoping he would stay around a little longer.

Vivian saw the shine of Rebecca's black Escalade peek between the sagging branches of the willows, before it rounded the corner of the driveway. The sun slipped just below the treetops, casting an orange glow across the sky. As the vehicle made the curve of the circle drive, Vivian closed her history book, set it beside her, and rose from the swing. Instinct made her hurry toward the top of the steps, where she stood as the vehicle stopped below them.

She saw her father in the passenger seat. James looked up at Vivian as Rebecca shifted the gear into park and almost simultaneously jumped from the driver's side door. Before he could push his own door open, Rebecca was pulling it open for him. His eyes looked so tired. His hair was uncharacteristically disheveled.

Rebecca reached for him and helped him out of the car. He blushed.

"I really can get out myself," he said, but he accepted her help with no other protest.

His back hunched slightly, Vivian saw the shadow creature slung around his shoulders like a thick, black blanket. Thane appeared behind him, watching the shadow closely, the creature glaring back at him.

As much as Vivian wanted to see her brother, she

avoided making eye contact with him out of fear that the shadow would notice that she could see him. She tried to watch him from the corner of her eye as he set his jaw and stared down the demon on their father's back.

James looked up the steps at Vivian, a small, hopeful smile raised his cheeks. Thane reached toward James, placing his palm gently on his father's back. The shadow creature pulled away from the touch and hissed.

Rebecca kissed James's cheek.

"Of course you can do it yourself, but you just spent the day in the hospital. Let me dote on you a little."

Thane glared at the creature still clinging to James's back.

"*Get off him,*" he demanded. "*Leave my dad alone!*"

The demon hissed and thrashed at the air. Thane kept his hand on his father's back and yelled. The intensity of his voice startled Vivian.

"*Get away from him!*"

The creature reared up into the air and screeched. The sound pierced Vivian's ears, but hung silently in the air around her father and Rebecca.

"It was just an anxiety attack," James protested.

"The doctor said your blood pressure was dangerously high. They don't keep you all day, connected to monitors for *just* an anxiety attack."

James took a step toward the stairs. His brow furrowed as he bent down, putting his hand on his knee as he caught his breath.

"Do you need to sit down?" Rebecca's eyes widened at his sudden display of weakness.

"I'm okay. I'm just…a little…tired."

Thane put both hands on their father's back. The demon hissed and clawed at James's shoulders, clinging to him.

"*Leave him alone!*"

Vivian watched her brother defending their father. For a moment she considered backing away into the house. She didn't want to see her brother fighting with a monster. She didn't want to watch her father buckle under the weight of the demon her anger was helping to feed. She wanted to look away. But she knew she couldn't hide from the demon in front of her, any more than she could hide from the demons lurking in the house behind her.

She hurried down the steps toward James and, looking into her brother's eyes, reached out and took her father's hand. It was the first time she had touched him in almost a year. A surprising warmth rose through her. Her father stood straight, his blue eyes glazed over with tears.

"Between the two of us, we can get him into the house," she said to Rebecca.

The demon shrieked and slid to the ground, completely letting go of James. It seemed to melt into the sidewalk behind him. Thane's eyes sparkled as he smiled.

"Of course we can," Rebecca beamed. "We are two strong women."

"Stronger than you know," Thane added.

James let them help him into the house and settle him onto the sofa in front of the fire Grant had made before he and his mother left. Rebecca propped a few pillows up for him to lean back on and slipped his shoes off. As he put his feet up on the couch, he gently squeezed Vivian's hand, looked into her eyes and said, "Thank you."

Vivian smiled slightly and nodded before letting go of his hand. "Marybeth made stew for us."

"Let's dish it up. We can put a few TV trays up and eat in here by the fire."

"I'll help you," Vivian offered.

"If you want to set up the trays, I'll grab the grub." Rebecca pointed toward the closet in the corner of the room. "The trays are just inside there."

"Okay," Vivian agreed.

Thane had entered the room with them and stood beside

their father, protectively.

"That shadow has been growing on his back since the first night we got here," he said, breaking the silence in Vivian's mind.

"I know."

"You did the right thing, Vivian. The weight of his guilt is making him physically weak."

"He created that guilt, not me." Vivian slid three trays from a rack in the closet and carried them across the room. James's eyes were shut as she approached. His face looked pained. He opened his eyes as Vivian set the tray near him, dark circles ringed them, and his flesh looked sullen and pale. He seemed to be aging before her eyes.

"He created it, but you have the power to make it grow."

"That's not fair!" Vivian set her jaw as she looked at her brother. *"His guilt is not my responsibility."*

"Take it from me, there is nothing fair about life or death."

Vivian instantly wished she could take those words back. *"I know. I'm sorry."*

Thane moved from his perch near his father to stand beside Vivian. *"You did the right thing out there. I always admired that about you as my big sister. You knew what you did would help him fight that demon off his back, if only for a while."*

Rebecca bounced into the room carrying a tray with three bowls of steaming stew, a plate of rolls and butter, and three tall glasses of milk. She dispersed the food evenly on the three trays and positioned herself at the end of the couch near James's feet.

"What I did, I did for you," Vivian thought, looking at Thane stubbornly.

"Whatever your motivation," he replied, *"you did the right thing."*

Vivian sighed out loud. Her father and Rebecca both looked up at her.

"Is everything okay?" Rebecca asked.

"Yes," Vivian replied. "I just can't wait to eat." *And I hate it when my little brother is right.*

She sat in a high-back chair near her father's head on the couch. When he reached for his stew, the bowl wobbled a bit in his hands, spilling broth on the tray. Vivian instinctively reached forward and stabilized the bowl in his grasp by putting one hand under the bowl. With her other hand, she moved the tray closer to the couch.

"Get used to it. I had a ninety-nine percent right-rate when I was alive, but this whole death thing is very enlightening. I'm pretty sure I'll be hitting a hundred percent from here on out."

As her father smiled and thanked her for helping him, Vivian bit her lip and forced a smile.

"Doing the right thing sucks when you're righteously mad at someone." She glanced at Thane as she settled back into her seat and spooned a bite of her stew.

Thane simply smiled knowingly, and then he was gone. Vivian sighed aloud again. Her father and Rebecca both looked at her.

"This is delicious," she mumbled, stuffing her spoon in her mouth.

She wanted to tell them about the events of the afternoon, but she figured her father had been under enough stress for one day. He didn't need to hear that his hateful, angry daughter had also ripped a hole in the basement wall and was fairly certain a demon or the devil himself might be after her.

Marybeth had shown her how to lock the basement door, and where the key was kept. She would wait until tomorrow to mention the hole in the wall, or any of the other events from the day. For now, she would enjoy her food and the peace of the crackling fire. And she would stuff Thane's words about her part in feeding the shadow of guilt that her father carried with him deep into the back of her mind. She would worry about that later.

SHE HAD LOOKED SO frightened when they'd found her in the basement. Her eyes were so beautifully wide with terror when she realized that she wasn't alone. They wanted to get close enough to look into those big, frightened eyes, but it wasn't the right time. Waiting was so hard.

"Be patient," they scolded themselves. "When the time is right."

They watched the family as they sat near the fire. The glare of moonlight on the window made it hard to see the details as clearly as they would have liked.

"Warm and cozy little family. Enjoy it while you can. Soon there will be one less person sitting down for family time." A hoarse giggle, gurgled through their lips.

CHAPTER TEN

THE PROJECTOR BUZZED. THE VIDEO, CIRCA nineteen-eighty-something, displayed on the screen centered on the whiteboard in the front of the room. Snickers rippled through the classroom as a woman with over-permed hair entered the scene. A clock ticked dully above the images as two speakers blasted the muffled voice of the big-haired woman, her words slightly obscured by the buzz of the audio.

Vivian struggled to focus on the video. Her chin was propped on her hand as she nibbled on her nails—a habit her mother had begged her to stop. Her mother had even painted Vivian's nails with polish that tasted like bitter dandelions. It made Vivian's eyes water, but she bit at her nails despite the unpleasant taste. Gazing thoughtfully at her torn cuticles and jagged, chipped nails, she felt the urge to stuff her hands in her pockets. Maybe she should stop. It was a nasty habit.

The crackle of the projector pulled Vivian's attention away from her scruffy nails. Glancing across the room, she saw the spirit of an old woman who stood beside a blonde girl sitting in the front row. The girl scribbled notes as she watched the movie intently. The old woman gazed proudly at her as she worked.

Another girl nearby, scribbled on a piece of paper too, but she never looked up at the screen. It did not take a sixth-sense for Vivian to be fairly certain her note had nothing to do with the movie they'd been instructed to watch.

Behind the note taker, a shadow perched on a boy's desk like a crow. The boy wiped his long hair from his eyes as he sat low in his chair and stared at the ceiling. The shadow was small, about the size of a basketball, and had the shape of a small, potbellied man. Pointy, gremlin-like ears perched high on top of its round, smooth head. Gnarled fingers tapped on the boy's chest as the tiny demon hissed, "*Loser*" in rapid succession. The boy sighed and clenched his teeth.

It amazed Vivian that people did not know the spirits were around, yet somehow seemed to hear them. The hateful words of the dark ones affected the souls of the humans they harassed, crushing their confidence and filling their thoughts with hate for themselves or for others.

Each shadow seemed to have an agenda. Their goal was to destroy the basic human potential of their host and drag them into a place as bleak as the blackness of their own forms. They murdered hopes and dreams and slowly hacked away, like tiny hatchets, at the self-esteem of their victims. Their presence made it all too easy for a person to believe the world might be better off without them.

On the other hand, some people had guardian spirits hovering around them. These spirits fed hopes and dreams with the light and peace they breathed into their loved ones.

Vivian couldn't help but wonder why some people got stuck with darkness clawing at their souls, while others got to tra-la-la through life, with sunshine beaming down on them. Life was so unfair. She had become the poster-child for exactly how unfair life could be.

Trying to look casual, she peered over her shoulder to see if Grant had his shadow friend tagging along with him today.

She didn't see a shadow, but she did catch Grant gazing at her. His eyes connected with hers as he flashed his perfect, toothy grin. Vivian felt her stomach flip as she returned the smile.

I wonder how long he's been looking at me! Her heart fluttered in her chest as she watched him hand a note folded into a tiny square to the girl next to him and point at Vivian. The girl adjusted her glasses as she peered at Vivian, then raised an eyebrow as she glanced back at Grant. Oblivious to her inquisitive look, Grant kept his eyes on Vivian.

The note traveled through the rows as one student tapped another's shoulder and pointed toward Vivian. Most of her classmates barely flinched as they complied with the request, but one girl, who Vivian recognized immediately as one of Hailey's fellow cheerleaders, glanced back to see Grant smiling at Vivian. She scrutinized Vivian with hate-filled eyes, before tapping the shoulder of the girl ahead of her. Her expression oozed with unfettered disgust, as she rolled her eyes while pointing at Vivian for the note to be passed forward.

Heat flushed Vivian's face as the note was slipped onto the corner of her desk. She glanced at Grant, then to Hailey's friend who still glared at her, then back to Grant who smiled broadly as she unfolded the sheet of lined paper and read, *Can I talk to you after class?* The letters were so neat, an elementary teacher could have written them. It figured. Even his penmanship was perfect.

Beaming, she looked back at Grant, who was watching her intently. His ever-present grin turned up a few notches when he saw her nod her head and flash a thumbs-up in response. The cheerleader's icy stare intensified. Vivian tried to ignore it as she looked back at the note on her desk. Her heartbeat quickened as she read it again.

The projector was still buzzing when the bell rang. Chairs screeched as the rustling of papers and zips of backpacks buried the muffled words of the actors on the screen. A mass of bodies rushed toward the hallway.

Vivian took her time putting her notebook and pen into her bag. She waited for the herd of chattering students to push through the opened door before following the pack.

Grant stood just outside the classroom, a poster of the Richfield High football team against his back.

"I think you might be leaning against your own face." Vivian laughed as he peeked over his shoulder.

"These things are everywhere," he replied, his cheeks blushing. "I guess they're trying to boost ticket sales or something. I'm not sure these ugly mugs will make people want to come to the game."

Vivian observed his features thoughtfully. There was absolutely nothing ugly about his mug.

"I had no idea your mom worked at my dad's house," she said, breaking a moment of awkward silence.

"She's been working at that house for as long as I can remember. I've practically grown up, running around out there."

"You probably feel more at home there than I do." She wanted to ask him about Sarah, but what she wanted to know would take longer than the four minute passing period would allow him to tell her.

"I suppose, I probably do," he said with a sympathetic smile. He shifted his weight slightly as his cheeks dimpled and turned a deeper shade of crimson. "I wondered if you have plans for lunch today."

"Well, I was planning to choke down just enough food to make it through the day without passing out from hunger. I haven't decided yet if I'll sit in the cafeteria and listen to people whisper about me or eat in the girl's locker room. I'm kind of leaning toward the locker room."

"I was going to ask if you'd like to have lunch with me, but you sound busy," he teased.

"Hmm...lunch with the school superstar, or lunch in the

locker room by myself. It's a difficult choice, but I suppose I could do the locker room thing tomorrow."

"I'll meet you at your locker, after fourth period." He moved away from the wall he'd been leaning against.

"My locker's over by Ms. Jensen's room," she said as they began to walk down the hallway together.

"Yeah, I know," he shot back as he turned the corner. He took a couple steps backward, gazing at her as if he was not quite ready to take his eyes off of her. "I better get to English lit. I'll see you in history!"

"Not if I see you first." She winked.

"Not if I see you first? Nice one, Grandpa!" Thane appeared beside her. *"Are you planning to do the old pull-the-penny-from-the-ear trick at lunch?"*

Heat rushed to Vivian's cheeks. *"I know, but he makes me so nervous I turn into a huge dork, whenever I even think about talking to him,"* she thought back.

"Well, then I'll have to sneak into class like a ninja so you don't see me before I see you." Grant winked back.

Her heart throbbed as she watched him turn and hurry down the hall.

"He's so dreamy," Thane teased with a smile.

"Pretty much."

"You better flutter off to class, love bird."

Vivian's smile threatened to split her cheeks as she hurried toward her next classroom. She knew Thane had disappeared as soon as she had taken her first step down the hallway. He flitted in. He flitted out. She was beginning to get used to it. She wished he could stay longer, but she could only try to be content with whatever little bits of her brother she could get. She knew she was lucky to get any at all.

Besides, she was too happy to be sad about anything at that moment. In about three hours, she would be having lunch with Grant. How could she be anything but happy?

She smiled dumbly through geometry, while Mr. Aboud

explained the reflective, symmetric, and transitive properties of congruence. She noticed the same girl from first hour glaring at her as she stared happily at the clock, willing the hands to spin faster. If every girl in the high school was giving her nasty looks, Vivian doubted it could shake her good mood.

Vivian Bennett was finally in a good mood. It had been a while since she'd been in one of those. For the first time in a few months, the sun was shining—metaphorically speaking—and Vivian was basking in the warm rays of happiness. It felt nice.

When the bell finally rang, Vivian practically sailed down the hall to art. She sketched the still life display in the center of the room while peering at the clock out of the corner of her eye. Her flowers were drawn halfway out of the vase in an awkward array, and the bowl of fruit in the center of the table was sketched cockeyed on her paper. Had it been a real bowl and not a drawing, the apples would have spilled onto the floor.

When the bell rang, Vivian dumped her charcoal pencil and art gum eraser into her tray and nearly knocked Mr. Wigley over as she rushed out the door. She tried to walk casually down the hallway toward fourth hour. Grant walked ahead of her, backpack slung over his thick shoulder. Two equally thick-shouldered boys walked beside him, laughing and high-fiving each other over Grant's head. Hailey stepped in front of the threesome, and planted herself directly between Grant and the door.

"We need to talk," she said. Her jaw set as she placed her hands on her slim hips.

Vivian slowed her pace as she saw a group of Hailey's friends standing in front of Mr. Wesley's door staring her down as she walked toward them. She tried to melt into the cluster of students entering the classroom. The girl from first and second hour looked her in the eyes as she passed and mouthed, "Whore."

"Not now, Hailey," Grant said, as he glanced sideways at Vivian entering the classroom. His fists clenched, when he saw one of them call her a whore.

"We can talk after school. Alone," he said, narrowing his eyes at the posse of cheerleaders surrounding them.

"Fine!" Hailey cried as she pivoted on her feet and walked quickly into Mr. Wesley's room just a few feet behind Vivian.

Vivian stared ahead as she moved toward her seat. She had the sense that someone was walking close behind her. Too close. As she turned to sit in her seat, she nearly hit Hailey with her backpack. Hailey stepped so close to Vivian that she could feel hot breath against her face. She could smell spearmint gum as Hailey narrowed her eyes.

"Stay away from my boyfriend." She spat the words out like daggers.

Vivian watched the black vapor that swirled around Hailey's body, wrapping her like a boa constrictor coiling around its prey. She wanted to tell Hailey to back off—that she could talk to anyone she wanted to talk to. But when she saw the shadow twisting around her, she bit her cheek to keep from talking.

Even though Hailey had been less than nice to Vivian, she couldn't help but feel sorry for her. She had watched that shadow swirl around Hailey since Vivian's first day at Richfield High. It was especially dark and strong. Vivian wondered how she would act if a shadow that strong was brooding around her.

After Vivian sat down, she removed her notebook from her backpack. She reached into the front pouch of her bag and pulled out a pen, while Hailey hovered over her.

"I don't know what's going on with you and Grant, Hailey, but I'm sorry if you think it has something to do with me."

"It has everything to do with you!" Her nostril flared as

she clenched her teeth tightly.

"Leave her out of this, Hailey." Grant stood in front of Vivian's desk. "This is between you and me. She has nothing to do with it!"

Hailey's cheeks flushed red as she glared from Vivian to Grant, then back to Vivian. "Your daddy might be rich, but you're nothing. You barely even have a family. You're just a nobody, who thinks she's better than everyone else. Your dad probably doesn't even want you around! He only let you move here because your mom and brother died!" The shadow swirled around Hailey's head. It's black, clawed fingers reached toward Vivian, scratching at the air as it seethed and hissed like an angry cat.

Vivian's eyes filled with hot tears as Hailey's words slapped her in the face.

"Hailey, that will be enough." Mr. Wesley's voice boomed from behind Grant. "I need you to go to your seat, or we may need to discuss a trip to Mr. Pratt's office."

Hailey looked down at her feet as she walked silently to her seat. Vivian stared at her desk, watching teardrops puddle on her notebook. Her head began to spin as she tried to hold back the sobs threatening to explode from her tightened throat.

"I'm so sorry, Vivian." Grant's voice sounded as if it had been trapped inside a tin can. Mr. Wesley hurried him to his seat, before placing a heavy hand on her shoulder.

"Vivian, would you like to visit the guidance counselor?"

She shook her head without looking up.

"Well, if you change your mind, or if you need a minute to yourself, you can just slip out of the room. No need to ask permission." He squeezed her shoulder gently before moving toward the front of the room.

She could sense the curious stares of her classmates, as she focused her attention on the small pool of tears which had collected on top of her red, spiral notebook. They whispered as they mulled over her unfortunate circumstances. Mr. Wesley's lecture silenced the whispers, but the feeling of their eyes on her continued throughout the hour, as the ticking of the wall clock kept time with her throbbing scar.

Harry kept his hands and strange looks to himself, for the first time since she'd sat next to him on her first day of school. He even refrained from picking at the scab on his right arm — his usual fourth-hour routine. Vivian wondered how long he'd had that sore and if it would ever heal. She supposed not, if he didn't stop picking at it.

As the bell rang to end fourth period, Jen slipped a piece of paper on top of Vivian's notebook. It said six simple words. *Sorry about your mom and brother.*

It wasn't anything eloquent or profound, but the gesture of kindness made Vivian's eyes moist with tears. She looked up and smiled at Jen who was peering down at her from behind her black curtain of purple-tipped bangs. Jen's tag-along shadow hovered quietly behind her shoulder, almost as if it were hiding.

"Thanks." Vivian stood up and slipped her backpack over her shoulder. She folded the note and rubbed the smooth paper between her fingers. "Really, Jen, you're one of the few people who've been nice to me since I got here. It means a lot. More than you know."

"No problem." She shrugged, looking slightly embarrassed that her gentle side had been discovered. The shadow hiding behind her shoulder appeared smaller than it had been just a few moments before. Its mouth opened as if it was trying to speak, but no sound came out.

"FYI, Hailey's in my P.E. class after lunch, and I'm pretty sure my volleyball might accidentally slam into her face while I'm practicing my serve. I'm so uncoordinated, sometimes stuff like that just happens!"

"Thanks, Jen, but you don't have to do that. Really, I'm okay." Vivian smiled, glad someone cared enough to have her back. The throbbing in her scar began to fade.

"Well, if the ball accidentally hits her, then it accidentally hits her." Jen shrugged her shoulders as she turned toward the door.

Vivian watched Jen walk out of the room. It felt good to know someone wanted to defend her. She wasn't completely alone. She walked quickly toward the door.

"Try to have a good day, Ms. Bennett," Mr. Wesley said sympathetically as he looked up from his desk which was positioned in front of the white board.

"Thank you. I'll be okay."

Although she spoke the words with an air of confidence that sounded convincing, even to herself, she did not believe them. She was pretty sure nothing would ever be okay again.

CHAPTER ELEVEN

GRANT STOOD JUST OUTSIDE THE CLASSROOM door. His shoulder pressed against the brick wall, as he tapped the back of his U.S. History book nervously. His usual dimpled smile flashed as he saw her exit the room, and he stepped toward her.

"Ready for lunch?" he asked, a hint of uncertainty straining his voice. "If you're still up for it."

"A girls gotta eat." Vivian winked.

Grant's shoulders relaxed as he let out a deep breath, releasing the tension that must have built up as he waited for her to exit the room.

"It's actually pretty warm out today, and I was kind of thinking maybe we could have a picnic."

"And give up having everyone stare at me while I eat? I think I can handle that."

They walked through the cafeteria together. Their bodies occasionally bumping into one another, as they squeezed through the crowd of gawking students. The steady roar of chatter dwindled to a low buzz as they exited the school through the wall of doors opposite the rows of tables filled with their rubbernecking peers.

Outside, the autumn air was crisp, and the breeze penetrated the thin cotton of Vivian's shirt despite the brightness of the sun. The faint scent of burning leaves replaced the greasy aroma of the cafeteria.

"It's a little chilly," Grant said, watching Vivian rub her arms with her hands. "Here."

Pulling his arms out of his jacket, he wrapped it gently around Vivian's shoulders.

Vivian could imagine the uproar behind the glass doors separating them from the cafeteria filled with students. She could feel the stares on her back as they walked toward the football field. As she melted into the warmth of the jacket, she breathed in the smell that clung to the collar—a mix of Irish Spring and cologne.

They walked without speaking—the breeze whispering through the blades of grass and rustling a few scattered clusters of dried leaves was the only sound to interrupt the peaceful silence of the afternoon. As they crossed the all-weather track, Grant jogged ahead. When he reached the fifty-yard line, he sat his backpack on the ground and pulled out a brown, paper bag and a white towel from the locker room. Spreading the towel on the ground, he set the bag in the center.

"Sorry," he apologized. "I didn't exactly have a picnic blanket in my locker."

"As long as you got this towel from the clean pile and not from the dirty one, we're all good."

Vivian sat on the yellowing towel, as Grant laid out lunch: peanut butter sandwiches, string cheese, apple juice boxes, and a package of Ho Hos's

"Lunch is served," he exclaimed dramatically as he made a grand gesture with his hands.

Vivian couldn't suppress a giggle as she watched him pull the straws off the sides of the juice boxes and poke them into the tops.

"I haven't had a juice box since I was like, ten."

"You're never too old for 100% fruit juice conveniently served in a little box. At least that's what my mom tells me when she brings them home from the store."

"You're mother's a wise woman."

"She is," he said thoughtfully.

She sipped through the tiny straw, while Grant bit into his PB&J. It was gone before Vivian swallowed her first bite. He sucked the juice out of the box until the straw gurgled up the last bits of liquid.

"I wish I could eat like a boy. You just inhaled your lunch in two minutes flat."

"Sorry. Bad habit. I've been told I should slow down and taste my food."

"By your wise mom?"

"Yes, same one." His cheeks flushed pink.

She liked the way he blushed, when he talked about his mom. Vivian gazed across the towel into his blue eyes, admiring how the sunlight made them sparkle. She had the sudden and rather strange thought, that if she made a picture of him in her art class, she would use blue glitter to color his eyes.

"How's your dad doing after his day in the hospital?"

"He seems okay. The doctors said it was mostly anxiety, but they're worried about his blood pressure. They said he'll be alright, though."

"Good." Grant paused. "My mom felt horrible about what happened in the basement."

"Yeah, that was kind of embarrassing. I mean, who freaks out and literally rips through a wall to escape?" She joked, trying to make light of the situation.

"Apparently, you do." Grant smiled.

"My dad's already had Raymond patch my escape route, so if I'm ever down there and become horrified again, I'll have to start from scratch."

Grant chuckled. "By the way, when Armageddon goes down, I want you on my survival team. Deal?"

"Deal." Vivian giggled.

They sat for a moment just smiling at one another. It was one of the moments when her brother would have shouted, "Awkward silence!" But there was nothing awkward about it.

"I really wanted to ask you something, but after everything that went down in Mr. Wesley's room, I'm afraid you'll say no." He bit his lip as he inspected the yellowing edges of the dingy towel.

"I'm not easily shaken. Seriously, it was no big deal."

"Well, I'm sorry anyway. Hailey can be brutal. I don't know why she thinks she needs to drag you into our mess."

"I can handle it. Really, I've handled worse things."

His eyes glistened as he returned her gaze sadly, almost as if they might leak tears if he blinked. She wished he'd stop looking at her like that. She was tired of everyone feeling sorry for her.

"Well, then, maybe you could handle this. I mean it could be pretty awful, but I was hoping you would go with me to homecoming."

"That sounds dreadful! But I think I could try to bear it," she teased with a wink.

His cheeks dimpled. "Then it's a date?"

"Sure. It's a date."

"We can go to dinner before the dance, if you want. I won't even make you eat off an old locker room towel."

"Can we have juice boxes with dinner?"

"I could probably make that happen."

Vivian peered up at the sky. A wisp of clouds wafted across the otherwise clear, blue horizon, as a light wind blew her hair off her cheeks. She probably couldn't have appreciated the absolute perfectness of the moment a few months ago, but as she looked back at the boy sitting across from her on a grungy P.E. towel, licking the chocolate smudges off his fingers while a trail of white cream dribbled down his chin, she appreciated every bit of it.

"You inhaled that Ho Ho in one bite, didn't you?" She shook her head as she feigned disgust while squeezing her lips together in an attempt to hold back her laughter.

Grant nodded his head, while flashing an opened-mouth grin, his teeth still coated in chocolate and cream. Somehow, he still managed to look incredible. Vivian grabbed the other Ho Ho and stuffed the entire thing into her mouth. She chewed with her mouth gaping open as much as possible.

"Mmmm...dis is ood!" she said. Bits of chocolate sprayed out of her mouth while she spoke, still chewing the cake.

Grant's eyes widened while he doubled over laughing. "You did not just do that!" he exclaimed, waxy, chocolate icing still stuck to his front teeth. "You are awesome!"

"You're not bad yourself," she said after rinsing her mouth with a drink of apple juice. She extended the box toward Grant. "Now, clean off those front teeth, or we're gonna have to change your name to Bubba and marry you off to one of your cousins."

He took the box and swished the juice around his mouth for several seconds.

"Did I mention that you're awesome?" he said, regarding her thoughtfully.

For a few moments, that was exactly how she felt. Awesome.

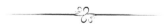

THEIR JAWS TENSED AS they watched the couple giggling and flirting with each other. The plan would be much easier if she remained isolated, but they had already known this little friendship would blossom. Grant was bound to like this one. He always liked them.

Their breath quickened as they folded their arms across

their chest. Their fingers clawed at the backs of their arms until the skin puffed into thin, pink lines, and tiny beads of blood rose to the surface. A low, steady growl quivered through their pursed lips.

"Enjoy her while you can," they hissed. "It won't be long before you can't enjoy her anymore."

CHAPTER TWELVE

"OKAY, THAT LOOKS TOTALLY HOT!" ANNA dropped her jaw dramatically as Vivian twirled in front of the mirror.

"Really? It's kind of...frilly." Vivian cocked an eyebrow, as she gazed thoughtfully at her reflection.

"It's homecoming, and you're a girl. It's kind of supposed to be frilly!" Anna smoothed the glittery, black overlay on the skirt of Vivian's dress. "Plus you look smokin'! Grant is going to flip!"

Homecoming was a week away, and Vivian had tried on every dress in the only formal shop in Richfield twice. But for some reason, she found fault in all of them. So she and Anna road-tripped to Alberleen, a slightly larger town about an hour south of Richfield.

"Okay," Vivian replied, as she spun around in front of the mirror one final time. "This is the one."

Anna squealed as she wrapped her arms around Vivian's bare shoulders. "Not that it hasn't been a blast watching you try on every dress from here to Richfield..."

"Twice," Vivian interjected, shaking her head in disgust as she gazed at her reflection in the mirror.

"Yes, twice! But it was worth it, because you look awesome! Besides, it got me out of Richfield for the day."

"It has been nice to have an excuse to get away from my dad's house. Sometimes I feel totally isolated from the world out there in the sticks."

"Try living there your entire life. Honestly, I felt a little badly about how excited I was when my dad told me you would be moving into the main house."

She shifted her weight as she looked thoughtfully at Vivian's reflection in the three-way mirror. "I mean, I was sad about why, but I was happy I'd have someone my own age around the estate again."

Vivian made eye contact with Anna's reflection in the middle panel of the mirrors. A light haze began to plume behind Anna's head.

"Sarah Christian and I both lived there our whole lives. We came home to the estate from the hospital as babies. She went to the main house, and I went to the back house—just a couple months apart. Then last summer, after her mom died, she ran off. I guess she just couldn't stand Richfield, or being stuck under her father's strict rules anymore. Her father was devastated when she left. He moved to their summer house on the East Coast six months after Sarah ran away. Said he couldn't live in that house alone anymore. I've spent every moment since she left wishing she would have taken me with her." Anna's voice trailed off to a whisper.

The hazy cloud that had formed behind her began to circle her body at a slow, but steady pace, darkening her features, causing her to look haggard and almost old. She gazed at the mirror as if she were looking through it to some far off place where Sarah had gone. A single tear slipped past the corner of her eye. She stopped its decent with the back of her hand.

Her eyes traveled back to Vivian in the mirror and she smiled warmly. "Then you came along." The shadowy cloud rose above Anna like a small tornado and disappeared into the ceiling. Then it was gone. Anna's haggard and tired expression left with the darkness. She looked young and happy again.

Vivian's stomach knotted as a small voice inside of her wanted to scream out that Sarah had not run away. She had the overwhelming thought Sarah's disappearance was linked to the pink room at the top of the stairs, and the dark spirit that seemed to be attached to it. She was also certain that Sarah's spirit had led her to the basement, although she wasn't quite sure why.

As she returned Anna's smile, she said, "Well, I'm glad we're stuck out in the sticks together."

After paying for the dress, Vivian carefully loaded the black, plastic bag into the trunk of her car. She tried not to obsess over the million questions she wanted to ask Anna about Sarah.

How had Sarah's mother died? How did they know Sarah had run away? Had anyone heard from her since she left? But Anna was clearly disturbed by the topic, and Vivian didn't want to bombard her new friend with questions about something that was so upsetting to her. She decided her questions could wait.

As she drove down Main Street, they passed the movie theater. The marquee showed one movie, *Alien Zombies*, at three different times.

"I guess if living-dead space creatures aren't your cup of tea, you're kind of out of luck on the movie choices for date-night around here." Vivian laughed.

"It doesn't sound like a very romantic date, but it's been so long since I've been on one, I'd probably go and pretend to like it," Anna replied with a shrug.

"I'd probably sit through any bad movie, if I could get a giant tub of movie theater popcorn. I'd even consider going with Harry Crap, if I was guaranteed a gut-full of that buttery yumminess," Vivian said.

"Eww!"

"Yeah, I like theater popcorn *that* much!"

"Oh, man, Chubby's!" Anna shouted, practically slobbering on the window as Vivian cruised past the red brick building. A small sign above a glass door read, "Chubby's Ice Cream."

"Do you need an ice cream fix?" Vivian asked.

"Yes, please! Do you need to hurry home?"

"Nope, my dad told me to take my time. And that was actually really fast."

"After all of our other shopping trips, he's probably not planning on you getting home until after dark."

Vivian laughed. "I *have* tortured you with all this dress shopping, haven't I?"

"That's what friends are for."

"Okay," Vivian made a sharp u-turn. "The very least I can do is get you some ice cream!"

Vivian slipped the car into park, after they'd coasted into a spot near the back door. As she shut her door and walked toward the ice cream shop, an extended-cab truck rumbled into the parking spot beside her BMW. The smell of diesel fuel burned her nostrils as a pack of boys rolled out of the front seat like a herd of circus performers spilling out of a clown car.

"Hey, Vivian!" Grant's voice came as such a surprise to Vivian that she stumbled over the front of her own foot, when she heard it. Grabbing Anna's arm to regain her balance, she glanced over her shoulder.

"Hey," she replied with a grin.

"What are two lovely ladies like you doing here?" Jason Bashly, his football number proudly displayed on his letter jacket, swaggered toward Vivian and Anna, looking them up and down like two prized sows at a livestock auction.

"Umm…getting ice cream," Anna replied, rolling her eyes. "You can stop looking at us like you've got x-ray vision."

"You know I don't need super powers to see what's

under that sweater. I've got my memories."

"You wish," Anna retorted with a glare.

"Knock it off, Bashly." Grant's tone was firm as he glanced at his friend. "Sorry, Anna, he won't admit it, but Jason can be kind of a baby when a girl breaks his heart."

"Ah, come on, man! Enough with the broken heart talk," Jason protested. His tone softened. "Sorry, Anna. You know I'm just messing with ya."

Anna's hard-set expression relaxed as she shrugged her shoulders. "You're forgiven, I guess."

Grant gazed at Vivian, seemingly unaware of anyone else around them. "We were just heading to the movie, but you can't pass Chubby's, without stopping."

"I've never been here, but ice cream is pretty hard to resist. Any place called Chubby's has to be good!" Vivian blushed as she realized she was staring at Grant's lips, thinking about kissing them.

Anna had slipped in with the group of boys as they'd entered the parlor, leaving Grant and Vivian alone in the parking lot. A light breeze made Vivian's ponytail sway behind her.

Vivian could see Anna and Jason sit down at a pedestal table, his arms rested on the table top. Her fingers twisted at stray strands of hair that had slipped out of her ponytail and fallen around her face.

Grant followed her gaze. "They dated for nine months last year. He still can't get over the fact that she dumped him."

"Huh." She watched them thoughtfully. "He doesn't seem like her type, but I guess I don't really know her all that well."

"Did you know she was a cheerleader?"

"Yeah, she mentioned that."

"Captain of the cheerleading squad dates the starting running back—that kind of thing never happened where you're from?"

"Captain? I knew she was a cheerleader, but I never knew she was the captain." She peered over her shoulder toward her new friend.

Jason flexed his muscles and kissed his biceps as Anna bit her lower lip and giggled. Vivian would have never pictured Anna liking a jock, let alone dating one for nine months. She pictured her as the kind of girl who would date a boy who played electric guitar in a garage band. But there she was, flirting with her ex-boyfriend, the jock.

"So what *are* you two doing in Alberleen?" Grant stepped closer to Vivian, closing the small gap between the two of them.

"Dress shopping," she replied, rolling her eyes. She stuck out her tongue as if she were trying to get a bad taste out of her mouth.

"Was it *that* bad?"

"Worse! But it's done now. And I found a really cute dress."

"I can't wait to see you in it." His eyes sparkled as he reached up and brushed a piece of loose hair behind her ear. For a moment she was mesmerized again by those glittering blue eyes.

Lowering her head, she peered up at him shyly. She wondered if he wanted to kiss her as much as she wanted to kiss him. His lips looked soft, and she found her breath coming faster, as she watched him lick them. She softly bit her lower lip as she imagined his wet, soft lips pressed against her own.

A vehicle blasted into the lot and screeched into a parking space beside them.

"What the hell are you doing, Grant?" Hailey's voice was shrill as she slammed the passenger door of the Land Rover she'd been riding in. A dark mass slithered behind her as she rushed across the parking lot—clawed hands wrapped around Hailey's leg like a small child hanging onto an ankle for a ride.

She stomped across the blacktop, oblivious to her demonic passenger.

Grant closed his eyes and took a deep breath before turning around to face her.

"I'm talking to a friend."

"Well, we all need to talk." Hailey's eyes were red and puffy. Vivian assumed she'd been crying. Her lip quivered as she looked from Grant to Vivian.

Vivian stepped back uncomfortably. "I should probably just let the two of you be alone." She turned to walk into Chubby's.

"Wait, Vivian." Hailey grabbed her arm. Her expression was pleading as she looked into Vivian's eyes. "Please. We need to talk! All of us!" The shadow slowly slid up Hailey's leg and stood behind her back. It towered over her, head cocked as it fixed hollow, blackened eyes on Vivian. It whispered words so quickly into Hailey's ear that Vivian couldn't understand them.

Vivian kept her gaze on Hailey as she watched the creature from the corner of her eye. When she placed her hand gently on top of Hailey's hand, her grasp loosened slightly.

"Whatever is going on between you and Grant isn't my concern. You guys need to talk, but I don't really want to be involved."

"Well, you got involved when you started messing with Hailey's boyfriend!" A tall, thin girl interjected from behind Grant. Vivian immediately recognized the classmate from her first and second period classes. Her glare matched those of the girls standing beside her.

"Hailey, please leave her out of this. We didn't break up because of her. We broke up because it wasn't working, and it hasn't been for a long time." Grant looked sadly at Vivian. "I'm sorry you're being dragged into this."

"It's okay." She looked from Grant to Hailey. "I'm sorry, Hailey. I'm really sorry for what you're going through. But I'd like to be left out of it." She gently removed Hailey's hand from her arm and walked into the ice cream shop.

Vivian sat at the pedestal table beside Anna and tried not to look over her shoulder at Grant and Hailey through the large window behind her.

"Here we go again." Jason shook his head. "We can't even get away from her when we leave town."

"She's a stalker," another boy added.

"That's pretty harsh, Matt." One of Hailey's friend's had entered the parlor and stood behind him. "They dated for three years. That has to mean something."

"Yeah, it means he's a slow learner," Matt replied.

"I don't know how she tolerated him and all of his loser friends that long." The girl's nostrils flared as she clenched her teeth.

"Well, she doesn't have to now, so why don't all of you just stop following us! This is the third time this weekend that you just happened to be where we are."

A thud against the window behind Vivian made everyone jump. The entire shop seemed to pause. Orange soda dripped down the glass as a plastic bottle spun on the sidewalk below the window. Outside, Grant looked at the window with surprise and then back to Hailey.

The glass door squeaked open as another one of Hailey's friends stuck her head inside. "Let's go, Nina," she called urgently.

Vivian looked out the window and watched Hailey storming away from the parking lot. Her shoulders shook as she jogged down the street; an indiscriminate mass of black hovered above her as she ran. One of her friends chased after her, as the other girls loaded back into the Land Rover and squealed out of the parking lot as angrily as they had come in.

Grant looked at his feet as he slumped through the doors and headed toward the bathroom. The group of football players that had spilled out of the truck earlier stood in unison. A crash rang through the closed bathroom door that sounded like a foot kicking a trash can. Jason put up a hand and moved away from the table.

"I've got this."

"Chicks are crazy," said a red-headed boy with golden freckles sprinkled across his cheeks.

"Hey," Vivian protested. "We're not all crazy!"

"Yeah, I'm pretty sure I didn't freak out when Jason and I broke up," Anna added.

"You broke up with him," said the boy. "And he went a little loco."

"Well, I had a boyfriend break up with me last spring, and the worst thing I did was decapitate him." Vivian paused dramatically. "By cutting his face out of my homecoming pictures." She shrugged her shoulders and smiled.

The crowd of beefcakes smiled back. A few laughed out loud. The bathroom door squeaked as Grant and Jason walked out.

Grant flashed an apologetic look at Vivian. "Sorry about…"

"Grant, don't worry about it!" Vivian interrupted him. "People throw soda bottles in my general direction all the time. Seriously—no big deal."

"Movie starts in ten minutes, dudes. We should probably split." A thick shouldered boy with glasses handed Grant a milkshake in a to-go cup. "Your usual, bro. Don't get brain freeze trying to suck it all down before the movie."

"Thanks, Rosco." Grant turned to Vivian. "Do you guys want to see *Alien Zombies* with us."

"Thanks, but zombies totally freak me out," Vivian replied. "Besides, you boys came to hang with the guys. No more chick interruptions allowed."

"Amen to that!" Jason patted Grant on the back. "I knew I liked you, Vivian."

"Thanks. I'm pretty sure I don't think you're a total tool

either, Jason." She winked.

Jason flashed a toothy grin at Anna. "So are we on for homecoming?"

Anna rolled her eyes, feigning disgust. "Sure. Why not?"

Vivian's eyes widened with surprise.

"I don't have anyone else to go with," she shrugged her shoulders and laughed.

"Well, I say we make it a double date, then," Grant interjected.

He leaned toward Vivian as his friends moved toward the door in a mini-football huddle, slapping backs and jabbering about zombies.

He touched the back of her neck, causing her skin to tingle like a jolt of electricity had been shot through her body, as he whispered in her ear, "Thanks for understanding, Vivian. I'm still sorry, but I'll try to make it up to you, somehow."

Her cheeks blushed as his lips brushed her ear. The minty fresh scent of his breath lingered as she watched him follow the group through the doors and into the parking lot.

Her heart pounded at her chest like a bass drum keeping time to a heavy metal band. Squeezing her eyes shut tightly, she willed it to slow down as she buried her face into her hands.

"Oh, girl! You've got it bad!"

Vivian's cheeks were warm as she peeked through fanned fingers at Anna. "He's so sweet, and cute, and funny, and…"

"Yes, Grant Jackson pretty much has it all. Except for a good dad. His father's as mean as they come."

"Really?" Vivian shifted in her seat as she leaned toward her friend. "I did notice that Marybeth seemed to have a black eye the other day."

"That poor woman always has a bruise somewhere. His dad drinks. A lot. And then he swings at anything that gets in his way."

"Even Grant?"

"Grant. His mom. The cashier at Quick Pump. He's been in jail so many times for fighting, I lost track years ago."

"Poor Grant."

"Luckily, he takes after his mom. She's one of the nicest people I know."

"She seems like it," Vivian agreed.

"And then there's Hailey; I think she's losing it," Anna said.

"She is a bit dramatic. Did she just throw an orange soda at me?"

"Pretty much. Those girls are pure drama. They were awful to Nancy, but when she died last year, they acted like they'd lost their best friend."

"The girl you said was killed in the bathroom?" Vivian pretended not to know for sure who she was talking about.

"Yes," Anna said. "Grant tried to break up with Hailey that summer. And he and Nancy started hanging out. Nothing serious. I think he was sort of exploring his options, and Nancy was a really sweet and fun person to hang around with."

"Grant dated Nancy?" Vivian asked in surprise.

"They never really had a chance to date. Before they could, Hailey convinced Grant to get back together with her. Seriously, if you'd blinked, you would have missed it, but to Hailey and her friends, Nancy had done the unforgiveable. But when she died, you would have thought they'd lost their best friend."

Vivian listened quietly. She could empathize with the cruelty of Hailey and her friends, and she was just seeing the tip of it. She could imagine the horrors they put Nancy through in the last few months of her life.

Anna paused as if she were traveling to a place deep inside her memories.

"We were warming up before the first football game of the season last fall. Nancy said she had to run to the bathroom. We were on the track practicing our stunts before the crowd got there. When she didn't come back, I went to tell her to hurry up..." Her voice trailed off as her eyes glazed over with tears. She stared past Vivian. Her face tightened as if she were looking at something that terrified her.

"Oh, how awful. You found her?"

"There was so much blood." Anna's voice had become monotone, her expression was almost trance-like. "Her eyes just stared at me, and her mouth was opened like she was screaming, but no sound came out."

Tears slipped down Anna's cheek as she stared ahead, as if watching the horror of that day on an unseen screen. "I guess I was screaming, because when Mr. Jackson pulled me out of the bathroom, everyone was standing there."

"I'm so sorry, Anna. That's horrible."

"I must have tried to help her. I don't remember. I just remember looking down and seeing her blood all over me. So much blood..." Her voice had become a whisper, and she closed her eyes trying to shut out the memory.

Vivian knew all too well there was nothing truly comforting she could say. She wrapped her arm around Anna's shoulders, which shook as she quietly cried.

Vivian cried with her for the innocence stolen from them both by death. There was a strange comfort in knowing she wasn't the only one who had looked death in the eyes.

It was a bond she wished they did not share.

CHAPTER THIRTEEN

A STARLESS SKY HUNG ABOVE AS her back pressed against the cold earth below. Her unblinking eyes stared into the night while a figure loomed a few feet above her motionless body. Only moments before, she had moved. She had struggled and fought against the hands of darkness. Now, her body was still.

Vivian saw through the lifeless eyes of this girl as dirt began to pile upon her bruised skin. A gentle wind rustled the slender, sagging leaves of a weeping willow that drooped above. The torn, light blue fabric of her nightgown draped across her body. Around her wrist was a thin, silver bracelet with a heart-shaped pendant resting on the back of her hand.

Vivian felt the chill of the moist soil as if it were falling on her own skin. Panic twisted at her mind, the way a person wrings out a wet towel, as she watched the contents of a shovel emptied over the girl's face—over her own face. She forced air through her nostrils as they became clouded with dust.

Through the grimy veil, Vivian saw a hand reaching toward her. She struggled to push her own hand out of the shallow grave, clinging to the arm of a woman who was silhouetted against the dense, night sky. Moonlight clouded her image with shadows, making it impossible for Vivian to see her clearly.

As she rose from the ground, the dirt falling from her face, she looked into the eyes of the woman who had pulled her from the deathbed. Vivian knew those eyes immediately. She recognized the touch of her mother, smoothing her hair away from her face as she kissed Vivian's forehead.

She tried desperately to hold on to her mother, but Vivian's body was pulled away as if by a vacuum—sucked toward the moonlit sky. She was pulled farther away from her mother, her hands pawing at the air as if she might be able to swim through the night, back into her mother's arms. Farther and farther away she floated—away from the disturbed earth covering the girl below a single willow tree amidst a vast forest of evergreens and oaks. Farther still, until the scene below her ascending body faded to black.

Slowly, Vivian awoke from her dream, and rubbed her fists into her eyes as she became uncomfortably aware of the sunlight streaming through her thin curtains. Her heart pulsed against the t-shirt she had slept in. Beads of sweat slipped across her forehead, dampening her hair, causing it to cling to her flushed cheeks.

She pushed the hair away from her face and peeked at her alarm clock. Seven forty-five—too early for a Sunday morning. She buried her head under her pillow and pleaded with herself to go back to sleep.

Restlessly, she stared at the inside of her eyelids and groaned in frustration as her mind began to race. She thought about the strange dream she had been pulled from. The vivid details spun through her mind. Her heart fluttered, as she recalled her mother taking her hand.

"God, why did you take my mom from me?" A sob followed her words, as she beat her fist into her pillow.

She hadn't prayed since the accident. She'd been too

angry. She'd cried out in anger at God many times, but she didn't consider that praying. Not the kind of praying her mother had taught her to do, anyway. A nice "thank you, Lord, for this and that", always followed by a "forgive me for my sins." Those were the kinds of prayers she had grown up saying.

Ultimately, she blamed herself for the accident, but somewhere in the back of her heart she allowed herself to share some of the blame with the one she knew could have prevented it. Didn't He control all things? That was what she had been taught, in the tiny yellow room in the back of her mother's church, while she sat around a wood-grained, metal folding table with a dozen other children.

It sounded so wonderful at the time, because they'd just finished singing "Jesus Loves Me". Surely, if Jesus loved her so much, He'd make sure life was good. At the very least, He'd never let anything truly tragic destroy her happiness. When you love someone you want them to be happy, right?

Wrong.

After the accident, she had thought about that a lot. Her conclusion was maybe Jesus simply did not love her as much as the song said He did. But the child who hid behind the disguise of a hardened sixteen-year-old, still clung to the hope of those lyrics. Even though, at this particular time in her life, she was not exactly feeling the love.

Her mother had encouraged Vivian and Thane to pray every day.

"It's the best way to reflect on what was good about this day and where you can improve tomorrow," she'd said.

Vivian was finding that more than a little hard to do. Every time she thought about talking to God, she wanted to scream at Him for letting such an awful thing happen to her mom. She wanted to ask why murderers and rapists were allowed to live on Earth, but her sweet kid brother, who dreamed of taking a mission trip to Africa when he graduated high school, was allowed to die. He never got to see Africa. He never even got to see the tenth grade.

She could not pray. Not now, anyway. For now, she could only scream at the sky and beat her fists into pillows. She would cry out the name of God in frustration, in some way confirming she had not completely given up the faith in His being. One day again, she hoped she would find herself ending her day with a heartfelt "thank you for this and that". But today she was not thankful. Today she was angry. Period.

Opening her eyes, she sat up against her headboard and pulled her knees to her chest. A cold breeze swept across her room, as if a window had been left open. Her eyes widened as she surveyed the space around her.

Shimmering sunlight danced across the wooden panels of her floor where the jeans she had worn the previous evening lay crumpled beside her bed. Her backpack sat unzipped on the chaise near the window, its contents spilling out. Everything seemed to be as it had been before, yet something felt different.

The house groaned quietly as the wind blew through the trees beyond her window, sending a scattering of dry leaves against the side of the house.

She closed her eyes as she rested against the headboard, trying to focus her thoughts away from her anger over her circumstances. A chill, like a cold breath, swept across her cheeks causing her eyes to snap open.

Then she saw her. Thin and pale. Standing by the window. A light blue, knee-length nightgown hung limply over her frail body. The lace, once stitched around the hem, had been torn away and hung like a noose beside her leg. Dirt caked her knee caps above her scrapped and bruised calves. Brown, shoulder-length hair hung around her cheeks, as her face tilted sadly toward the floor, brown eyes peering up at Vivian.

It was the girl in the dream she had just awoken from.

She had dreamt about her before—the night she had also dreamt of Nancy. This was the same girl who had been chained to Nancy in the field. She had seen a glimpse of her in the unformed entity that led her into the basement. There she stood, a full apparition as solid as any living girl.

Vivian rose from her bed, steadying herself against her mattress, as if holding onto something solid might ground in her in reality, despite the nightmare she found herself standing in the midst of.

The girl's thin arm slowly rose from her side and pointed toward the window. Although the windows were shut, the sheer curtains billowed gently.

"Who are you?" Vivian's voice slipped past her lips in a shaky whisper. "Are you Sarah Christian?"

Dirt smeared the creaminess of the ghostly girl's pale cheeks, and her dried, cracked lips trembled. With quavering hands, she touched the deep purple bruises that circled her thin neck just above her collar bone.

The air in the room became frigid as the girl opened her mouth to speak. A light huff passed through her lips, as a single tear trailed a muddy stream down her dirt-stained cheeks.

"Can you speak?" Vivian asked.

Slowly, a black mist seemed to rise from the floor and swirl around the girl. Her eyes grew wide with fear as the fog wrapped around her body like a snake immobilizing its prey. The thick, murky mist grew into the form of a large man, towering over the petite girl. She flickered as her image began to fade. The shadow figure seemed to swallow her into the blackness of its body, then turned toward Vivian and floated across the room until it was only inches from her face.

She gaped at the mass in horror. There was no hiding that she could see it. It was too late to look past it and pretend not to know it was there. Ember eyes shown from the black, wispy body, and a mouth, larger than Vivian's entire head, opened, baring the long jagged teeth of a piranha.

"She's mine," it hissed. The smell of rotting flesh rolled from its snarled mouth.

The dark beast slowly circled around Vivian, so close that its hot, rancid breath made her recoil in disgust. After completing a full roundabout of her body, it stopped inches from her face and screeched an inhuman howl that made Vivian squeeze her eyes shut and grab her ears. When the shrieking ceased, Vivian slowly opened her eyes. Her room was empty.

Dropping to her bed, she quivered as she stared in disbelief at the spot where the ghost girl had been standing. The sun glimmered off of something smooth and shiny resting on the wooden floor. Timidly, Vivian slipped off her bed and moved across the room, peering in every direction—fearful the dark beast might be lurking behind her dresser or hiding under her bed.

With trembling hands, she slowly reached down to pick up the object. A smooth, silver bracelet with a thick heart charm dangled from her fingers. She turned the bracelet around in her hands. Bits of dried dirt plugged the links of the chain. Vivian rubbed at the dirt on the charm. Engraved on the back of the heart, she read, "Sarah".

The dark spirit knew she had seen it. She could no longer pretend she was unaware of their presence. With the bracelet gripped in her fist, her jaw set firmly, she hurried toward her bedroom door.

She had to face them now. She had to be strong. She walked steadily down the hallway toward the staircase.

Pausing briefly at the landing, she breathed a determined breath and straightened her shoulders. Fear was her enemy. The shadows would feed on it.

"I'm not afraid of you," she murmured. Crossing the top of the steps, she turned the doorknob of the bedroom that had been closed up since her first night there. This had been

Sarah's room. She was not sure how she knew, but she felt it deep within her soul. If she wanted to fight whatever darkness was in her new home, she was certain she had to start here.

"*SHE CAN SEE US,*" the creature hissed into their ear.

They felt on edge, but they didn't know why. All they could think about was that girl. Vivian. The smell of her hair—strawberry shampoo. The way her nose crinkled when she laughed. The thought of her usually made them smile. But now they were agitated. Their fingers tapped incessantly against the arm of the rocking chair.

The shadow figure circled the small room, its clawed toes clicking against the floorboards as it paced. "*I don't like seers. They're trouble.*" A trail of mucus dripped from the blackened lips of the creature as it bared needle-sharp teeth. "*She has to die.*"

"Vivian, Vivian, Vivian," they chanted. Their heartbeat quickened each time they spoke her name. "So pretty. So sweet." They liked her. She was spunky and so full of life. Why couldn't they shake the urge to watch that life fade from her eyes?

"*Kill her!*" The hot breath of the demon sprayed phlegm into the air as it rose from the floor, hovering just above the human's body. "*She must die!*"

Suddenly, they could not stop thinking about killing her. How would they do it this time? Stabbing had been so messy. Choking was nice because they could watch the final breath slip past her lips as the lack of oxygen tinged them blue, but it had been over too quickly last time.

No. For Vivian they had other plans. They wanted to play with her. She was just too special to kill quickly. This time they would savor the game.

CHAPTER FOURTEEN

THE DOOR FELT HEAVY AS VIVIAN pushed it open. Flecks of dust swirled through the beams of sunlight shining through the opened shades of the window, making the room feel alive. Wooden floorboards groaned beneath her feet, as she crossed the room with more confidence than she truly felt and sat on the edge of the bed. Her body sank slightly into the softness of the feather-filled comforter as the chilled air, thick with an ominous energy, made the hairs on her arms bristle.

As she surveyed the room, she rubbed her forearms, trying to warm the prickled flesh. The layout of this room was much like her own down the hall. The headboard of the queen-sized bed was pushed against the wall near a six-paneled door which Vivian assumed led to a closet, as the one near her own bed did. Rather than a chaise lounge, the window nook contained a built-in window seat with pink and white striped fabric covering the cushioned bench. Pale pink curtains, tied back with white fabric bows, were draped on either side of the paned window, overlooking the same trees and shrubs that Vivian's bedroom towered above.

By all appearances, it was the perfect room for a girl. The

pale pink flowered paper covering the walls reminded Vivian of a dollhouse her grandmother had kept in her attic. As a very young girl, she had wished she could shrink herself and live in it. However, despite the soft colors and quiet beauty of this room, Vivian struggled to fight the overwhelming urge to run from it.

She sat silently as she glanced around the room, searching for any signs of the shadow that had been there the night she'd arrived. Though the air felt electric with an otherworldly energy, the shadow was nowhere to be seen.

Rising from the bed, she crossed the pale pink shag rug centered in the room and sat on a spindle-back chair tucked beneath a white desk. She thrust open the single drawer centered between the pairs of thin white legs just beneath the desktop, and peered inside. It was empty. Slipping her hand into the drawer, she felt the grainy wood on the underside of the desktop.

Bending down, Vivian looked under the desk, sliding her hands against the wooden frame as she searched. She found nothing. Abandoning the desk, she moved to the shiny, white dresser on the adjacent wall of the room, and yanked each drawer out, feeling inside and under each one. She had no idea what she was hoping to find. She was just compelled to look, hoping that when she found it—whatever it was—she would know.

As she pushed each drawer back into the dresser, the air around her became more frigid, until her body started shaking from the cold. White puffs formed in front of her as her breath quivered past her lips. The room pulsated with energy, and Vivian had the sudden sense she was being watched. Spinning on the backs of her heels, she glanced behind her.

Although the room looked empty, Vivian was certain someone or something was there, lingering just beyond perception. It was the sense that observes the world beyond sights and smells, past the sounds and tastes of the here and now, far away from anything that could be touched with flesh—that sense assured Vivian she was not alone.

Just past the bed, the closet door stood slightly opened.

"That wasn't open when I came in." She might have been speaking to herself as people often do. Or maybe she spoke to the person or thing lurking in a hidden place just beyond her sight.

Her footsteps echoed on the floorboards as she hurried toward the door. Pulling it fully open, she glanced inside. It was empty, except for a few dozen bare, metal hangers strung along the bar stretching from one side of the closet to the other.

In the middle of the wall behind the metal bar, was a wooden panel in the shape of a tiny door with a pewter knob centered at the bottom. She grabbed the knob and pushed the panel up, making it nearly disappear into the plaster above.

Vivian stared into an empty shaft gaping in front of her. A series of pulleys hung from above and disappeared into the deep blackness below. Leaning into the opening, she squinted into the dusty darkness of the hole and saw the cords of the pulleys attached to a platform of faded wood.

"A dumbwaiter." Her voice ricocheted through the empty space above her, shaking loose bits of dust that sprinkled through the tunnel like tiny, gray snowflakes.

There had been a dumbwaiter in the hallway of her mother's old apartment that connected their unit to the laundry room in the basement. Thane had often said he wanted to ride it down the four stories through the walls, but his mother had threatened to ground him for life if he tried it. If he had known how short a time that would actually be, maybe he would have risked it.

She pushed her hands through the cobwebs hanging loosely around the ropes and pulled down on one side. A screech echoed through the empty shaft as the wooden box slowly creaked from where it sat. Dust lofted into Vivian's eyes. With one hand, she rubbed at them while pulling on the rope with the other.

The lid of the cupboard slowly came into view. Dusty panels, which had once been stained to match the woodwork of the bedroom, were cracked and faded. Pellets of mouse droppings scattered across the peeling wood, rolling around like tiny, brown Tic-Tacs. As the top of the dumbwaiter rose past Vivian, an odor wafted from the inside of the cupboard — a mixture of musty wood and the same familiar, metallic scent that had overwhelmed her when she had first entered the house.

She peered into the box. Rust-speckled nails popped through the wood, their grip loosened by time.

That smell—it was so familiar. The kind of familiar that haunted her like a boogeyman in the closet, hiding behind hanging clothes and stacks of toys and stuffed animals. Out of sight, but always there. Breathing quietly. Wanting to be seen, but waiting for the perfect moment to reveal itself.

Her thoughts spun, as she tried to place it—flipping through scattered memories. Scraped knees and bitten lips flashed into her mind, but didn't quite click with the odor. She breathed deeply, trying to fill her senses completely with the scent.

Then she remembered. It struck her like a bitter slap across her cheek, only the pain penetrated much deeper than the surface of her skin. It was the type of memory you push down as deeply as you could, and prayed that it didn't rise to the surface ever again.

Her mind flung her back into the bent passenger seat of her mother's car. Shards of glass dripped from her hair like water after a shower. She could feel bits of glass stuck inside her right ear—the result of turning her head reflexively to the left when she realized they were just moments from colliding with the truck that sped toward them. She felt a trail of wetness slip down her forehead. It waterfalled over her eyebrow and dripped through her lashes.

Through the blur of the blood, Vivian could see her mother's head laying face-down beside her on the middle of the bench seat. Blood puddled on the faded upholstery.

"Mom."

Vivian's voice was a whisper against the sound of a horn blaring steadily. Her head pulsed with a pain like nothing she had ever imagined. The blasting horn was like a hammer, pounding against the fresh wound which had caused a stream of blood to cascade down her forehead.

"Mom," she repeated as she reached toward her mother's long brown hair. The interior of the car began to spin, and Vivian pulled her hand back to cradle her throbbing head.

The endless blare of the horn made her ears buzz as she pleaded with God to make it stop. She thought it must have been the driver of the truck. Maybe he had lost consciousness and collapsed against his steering wheel. Maybe he had died. The thought made her heart pound with panic. The idea there might be a dead body that close to her was terrifying.

Her ears buzzed with the incessant scream of the horn as she peered toward her mother. The sound became muffled as she lifted her head slightly, trying to look through the driver's side window. The glass in her right ear rattled as it shifted.

It was then that she realized it was not someone else's horn. It was their horn. Her mother's body lay slumped against the steering wheel, her chest pressed against the plastic button responsible for initiating the painful blast of noise.

The next few seconds of Vivian's life seemed to move in a kind of slow motion that only exists in movies. As she looked from the steering wheel to the middle of the front seat, the realization that her mother's head rested too far from her shoulders was a concept Vivian could not quite process.

She could see it. She knew what it meant. Yet she continued to call out to her mother. As if calling out her name enough times might make her less dead.

She cried out to Thane for help, but there was no answer.

Craning her neck, she peered into the backseat where, a few minutes before, Thane had been complaining that he was going to get his first tardy of the year, because they'd had to turn around to get Vivian's homework. Only, there was no backseat.

The back of the station wagon had crushed into a concrete barrier, folding the back of the vehicle into itself. The metal frame of the back window, which now held nothing but a single shard of glass dangling from the upper corner, was only a few inches from where Vivian sat. The place where her brother had been sitting was no longer big enough to hold a fourteen-year-old boy—at least not a fourteen-year-old boy who was alive.

The world faded to black, as the sound of the horn dissolved into silence. But the smell stayed with her as she entered a state of semi-consciousness and clinical shock.

It was a smell her mind had desperately tried to suppress. It was the stench of death. And death was the smell wafting from the gaping shaft in front of her now. The same smell that greeted her when she had first entered the house.

As Vivian's eyes adjusted to the darkness of the dumbwaiter, she looked deep into the corners. In the shadows, clinging to the tip of a nail, hung a small clump of brown hair. Vivian reached in and pulled it loose.

As she held the hair in her palm, the image of the ghost girl she had just seen in her bedroom flashed into her mind. Except in the image, she was not a ghost. Her body rested in the dumbwaiter, curled tightly in on itself, knees pushed against her chest. Her unseeing eyes, the blue of a cornflower, stared at the inside of the cupboard as the ropes and chains squeaked against the weight of her body, and the dumbwaiter slowly descended into the darkness of the shaft.

"Vivian?" Her father's voice pulled her away from the image. He stood beside her, his hand on her shoulder. Startled and bewildered, she looked at him, wondering how long he had been standing there.

"What do you see?" he asked, his voice almost apologetic. He looked at her sympathetically.

Vivian pulled away. "What do you mean?" She backed away from the closet, the clump of hair still clutched firmly in her fist.

"You see something," he said. "I'm your father, remember? I was there the first time you saw a spirit."

Vivian remembered the first time she could recall seeing a spirit. It was a memory untouched by her thoughts for so many years, she had all but forgotten that her father had been present.

She was four years old, and they had just returned home from visiting Grandma May at the hospital. Grandma May had been sleeping when Vivian sat beside her bed and kissed her frail, liver-spotted hand. Her breath hissed in short bursts like the air being let out of a balloon.

Vivian's mother had cried the entire car ride home. Her father sat silently, holding her mother's hand. It was one of the few moments she could remember him being tender toward her. Thane slept in a baby seat beside her as she slumped against her seatbelt, hugging the pink teddy bear the nurses had given her at the hospital, while the doctor spoke to her parents. The antiseptic smell of the hospital room clung to her clothes.

When they had gotten home, Vivian sat at the kitchen table, her black Mary Jane's swung a foot above the gray-and-white tiled floor beneath her seat. The pink bear had been propped up beside her bowl of marshmallow cereal. Hunched over in the chair beside her, his elbows on the table, face cradled in his hands, sat her father.

Normally, sugary cereal for dinner would have been a special treat. That night, she did not feel much like eating them. Despite her young age, she understood dinner went unmade because her parents were sad. Although she did not completely understand their sadness, it covered her like a thick, woolen blanket—too heavy and a little itchy against her flesh.

She twirled the marshmallows with her spoon, pushing them under the milk, which had turned a bleak shade of gray as the colors bled from the pink hearts, yellow moons, orange stars, and green clovers.

As she poked a heart with her spoon, she breathed through her nose. The familiar scent of stale cigarette smoke and lilac perfume made her smile. Vivian glanced up and saw Grandma May standing beside her.

"Pop," Grandma May giggled as the marshmallow sprung above the milk. Vivian giggled too. She pushed a clover shaped marshmallow under.

"Ploop," Grandma May poked Vivian's nose as she made the sound.

"Poop!" Vivian said back, laughing. Grandma May let out a deep, belly laugh that made Vivian laugh more.

"Why did you say that?" her father asked, raising his head from his hands.

"Grandma May said 'ploop'. It sounded like poop," Vivian replied still giggling.

"When did Grandma say that?" her father peered at her through bleary eyes. Her mother walked into the room, pausing in the doorway as she listened.

"Just now," Vivian replied.

"Vivian Ann Bennett, that is not funny." Her mother's voice was stern, but quiet—like she lacked the energy to raise her voice above a loud whisper.

"But, Mommy..." The ringing phone interrupted Vivian's protest. Her mother moved quickly across the room, as if answering the phone before it rang again would prevent the walls from crumbling down around them.

"Hello? Yes, this is she," she spoke quickly into the

receiver. Those were the only words she uttered before her shoulders began to shake, and Vivian's father took the phone from her trembling hands.

Grandma May sat in the seat her father had just abandoned. She wrapped her thick arm around Vivian's tiny shoulder. Her mother sobbed into her father's shoulder as he mumbled something into the receiver and hung the phone on the wall.

"Why's mommy crying?" Vivian asked, peering into her grandmother's bright green eyes.

"I'm going up to Heaven to be with Grandpa," Grandma May replied.

"I'm sorry, Vivian. Grandma May passed away." Vivian heard her father's voice, but her attention was focused on her grandmother, who sat beside her, tenderly embracing her. Vivian was not afraid or even very surprised to be seeing her grandmother's spirit. As Vivian looked back to that moment, she realized this was probably not her first encounter with ghosts. It was just the first she could recall.

Grandma May hugged Vivian tightly. "I can't stay long, honey. But I'll be back to visit you, if the Lord will let me."

As Vivian pressed her head against her grandmother, she was struck by the easy rise and fall of her chest. The wheezing Vivian had become so accustomed to hearing was gone.

"You don't rattle when you breathe anymore, Grandma." Vivian smiled. Vivian had always been afraid she could catch Grandma's rattle, like she could catch a cold from someone who failed to cover their cough.

"No, sweetie, my lungs are as healthy as a newborn babe's."

"Vivian?" Her mother had stopped sobbing and was kneeling beside her, watching her intently. Wiping at the tears trickling down her cheeks, she asked, "Can you see Grandma May?"

"Yes, Mommy. You don't see her?" Her mother smiled

and shook her head as fresh tears trickled from her eyes.

"Your mother can't see like you can. But she knows about your kind of sight. She always thought I was a crazy woman talking to invisible houseguests—only they weren't invisible to me. I knew you'd see me, though. I've known it since you were a baby."

Grandma May kissed Vivian's cheek as she rose from the chair.

"I have to go, sweetheart. I love you."

With those final words, Grandma May vanished, just as quickly as she had appeared.

Twelve years later, hundreds of miles away from the kitchen where her mother had first acknowledged her ability to see spirits, Vivian stood in front of her father—the truth of her gift spoken aloud, once again. She did not want to tell him anything, but the thought of facing alone whatever darkness possessed this house, terrified her.

"Please, Vivian. If you see something, you need to tell me. I'm your father."

"You're my father? Sure, but only when it's convenient for you!"

Vivian rushed from the room, still clutching the hair, too filled with anger to allow him to be her ally. She would rather be on her own.

The slam of her bedroom door shook the walls as she tried to shut out her father's voice calling after her.

I don't need him! she thought. *I'll never need him!*

CHAPTER FIFTEEN

THE TEAL TRAY CLATTERED ON THE TABLE, as Vivian clumsily sat down. Her hair was pulled back in a loose ponytail. Stray strands fell over her eyes as she propped her elbows on the table and let her head cradle in her hands. Although she sat in the middle of a crowded cafeteria, she still felt completely alone. She was too tired to care that most of her schoolmates were whispering and staring in her direction. She'd almost gotten so used to it; she barely noticed, even if she wasn't completely exhausted and distracted by her thoughts.

Her weekend had been plagued with nightmares. Images of death haunted even her waking moments. The dark energy seemed to linger in the background just beyond her perception, each moment she was in that house. And she had to admit that it was beginning to take a toll on her.

"Seriously, that was a killer tackle." She heard Grant's voice before she saw them.

"I'm still feeling it." Jason groaned.

Grant slipped casually into the chair beside Vivian as Jason turned a chair across from them so the back touched the edge of the wood-veneer table and straddled the seat. Vivian looked up to see Jason chug the contents from his milk carton in one head tilt.

"You look like crap," Jason said, dropping the empty carton onto his tray.

"Thanks," Vivian mumbled, slipping the loose hair behind her ears, suddenly self-conscious. She wondered for a moment if she really looked as badly as she felt.

"Ignore him." Grant winked. "He took a hard hit to the head at football practice this morning. I think it's affecting his vision."

"I mean, you're still a hotty, no doubt, but you look like you haven't slept in a week."

"You do look tired," Grant agreed, eying her thoughtfully.

"I am," Vivian admitted. "I suppose I'm still getting use to sleeping at my dad's house."

"I bet that old place is haunted," Jason interjected, dipping a limp French fry in a large puddle of ketchup that nearly filled an entire square of his tray.

A gray haze began to ooze across the cafeteria floor. It seemed to be coming from the hallway leading to the athletic wing of the school. Vivian watched the cloud pause a few feet behind Jason. It slowly began to rise and take the shape of a tall man. Vivian's eyes widened as the figured reached at least seven feet tall.

"Shut up, man. You're going to freak her out." Grant glared at Jason in disgust, before turning his attention back to Vivian.

She looked away from the shadow figure now looming behind Jason's head and tried to focus on his eyes when she spoke. "Do you think it's haunted because of Sarah?" The tightness in her voice made the dead girl's name come out with a squeak.

"No. Sarah ran off to get away from her old man," Jason replied, still chewing a fry. "Her mom died there, though."

"In the house?" Vivian asked in shock.

"Yeah. She had cancer, so it wasn't like a grisly murder or anything, but still, that house is so old. People always died at home in the old-days. Sarah was constantly talking about hearing footsteps and noises when no one else was home."

"Seriously, Jason," Grant said in a hissed whisper. His teeth clenched as he glared at his friend. "Shut up."

The shadow figure lurched toward Vivian, causing her to push herself away from the table. The hollow sockets where eyes should have been stared at her while the creature only she could see or hear shrieked.

"You're going to die."

The words rattled her brain as she scrambled back in her chair further, causing it to tip over backwards. Grant grabbed her by the shoulders before she fell with it.

"Vivian, settle down. Jason's just being a jerk. Your dad's house is not haunted."

She put her hands on his chest as she steadied herself. He wrapped his arms protectively around her, just as the shadow creature began to swirl around the two of them, wrapping them in a dark, tornado-like cloud of evil.

It didn't matter to Vivian that every eye in the cafeteria had been trained on the spectacle of her knocking her chair over. She didn't even notice the glares from the table where Hailey sat, surrounded by her cheerleading friends. The only thing Vivian saw was the blackness that threatened to swallow her.

"I have to get out of here." She gasped as she broke away from Grant's embrace and rushed through the swirling shadow figure. A shiver rattled through her body as she passed through the chill of the evil spirit, before running toward the wall of doors leading to the back of the school.

Grant rushed behind her. He beat her to the door and pushed it open.

"I'll come with you," he offered as she stepped through.

Vivian looked around to make sure the shadow creature had not come outside with them. In the cafeteria, Jason sat alone, watching them walk away from the school, a look of genuine shock etched across his face. Only he wasn't exactly alone. The dark cloud had rematerialized into a tall, man-like beast and stood behind him, following his gaze toward Grant and Vivian as they hurried away from the school toward the football field.

Vivian broke into a run, propelled by a fear she'd never felt before. The creature had spoken directly to her. It had threatened her life. She'd always been aware of the dark forces, seen them lingering on others around her, but they'd never threatened her. One had never spoken to her until now.

She wondered if it was the same demonic force that had been in her room with Sarah's spirit. Had the creature followed her to school? Was she now being stalked by Hell itself?

Vivian stopped running and bent over with her hands on her knees. She was aware of Grant standing beside her, but she didn't look at him. His labored breathing matched her own, as she tried to catch her breath. When her breathing finally returned to a controlled rhythm, she stood up and realized where she had run to.

She stood just inches from the bathroom door down by the concession stand, the padlock secured through the links of chain strung through the handle. She reached out and placed her hand against the cool, steel door. At the same moment a small, pale hand seemed to reach through the metal, pressing lightly palm to palm against Vivian's. Vivian could see the ghostly image of Nancy looking back at her.

"Vivian?" Grant's voice was just above a whisper. "Why did you come here?"

"She needs help," Vivian replied without looking away from the sad eyes of Nancy's spirit. "I have to help her."

Grant placed his hand gently on her shoulder. "I don't

understand." His voice was gentle, and although there was a tone of confusion in it, Vivian sensed that it was just that—confusion. Not disbelief, just confusion and concern.

"I wish you could see her." Vivian's gaze still locked onto the sorrowful eyes of the girl whose spirit seemed to be trapped in the horror of her own death. Vivian wondered how many times she had relived her murder locked behind this rusting door. "She looks so sad."

"You can see Nancy?"

Vivian turned to look at Grant, her hand still on the door pressed palm to palm with the hand of Nancy's spirit. His blue eyes glistened as he looked back at her. Confused and concerned, but believing.

"I'm touching her hand."

Grant blinked, as a tear slipped over his lower lashes. He reached toward the door and placed his hand on top of Vivian's. In the same moment, a cold, black wisp of shadowy, claw-like fingers reached through the door and clutched Vivian's wrist. Vivian pulled away with such force she fell onto her butt, taking Grant down with her. Another black arm reached through the door toward them, before both arms wrapped around the slim, fading image of Nancy, pulling her back into the cold, dark bathroom. She shrieked as she disappeared through the steel door.

Grant stared at the door in awe. His eyes wide with terror.

"Wh…what was that?" he stammered.

"You saw it?" Vivian asked, shocked that Grant had seen the shadow figure.

"I don't know what I saw. Like…black arms…or something." Grant's eyes were pleading. "What was that thing?"

Vivian scrambled to her feet and reached down for Grant's hand. He let her help him up. He was still shaking. She hugged him tightly as they both looked toward the door.

"I'm not sure exactly what it is," Vivian replied. "I think it's a demon or some kind of evil spirit. Somehow, it's trapped Nancy's soul here...I think...I don't know...I'm trying to understand what she needs from me."

Vivian's cheeks flushed. She was babbling. She wasn't even making sense to herself. She could only imagine how insane it all sounded to Grant.

"You probably think I'm nuts."

"I might have, if I hadn't just witnessed a pair of black arms reaching through a solid steel door. So if you're nuts, I guess I am, too."

"Hey, you two love birds, get back to the school!" Mr. Jackson shouted from below the bleachers. A pack of students jogged onto the all-weather track behind him and began the trek around the circle.

"Sure thing, Mr. J!" Grant gave a small wave before taking Vivian's hand and walking toward the school.

His hand felt warm and his grip was strong, yet gentle at the same time. They walked in silence up the grassy hill toward the back of the school. Grant stopped behind the shade of an old tree. Still holding Vivian's hand, he turned and looked at her. Silence hung between them for what felt like several minutes, although Vivian knew it had only been a few seconds. She couldn't read what he was thinking.

"Please don't tell anyone." She shifted her weight from one foot to the other as she tried to read his expression.

"I won't." He took her other hand. "I promise." He pulled her closer until her forehead touched his chin. His breath warmed the top of her head. He reached up and tilted her chin so she looked up at him. His expression was serious, his eyes, deep pools of blue that seemed to sparkle in the sunlight, looked worried. Then his lips touched hers. Soft. Just a light kiss. More protective than seductive.

"I have no idea what that was down there, but I promise to help you. Whatever it is Nancy needs from you, we'll figure it out together."

CHAPTER SIXTEEN

VIVIAN'S BACK PRESSED AGAINST THE CONCRETE bricks of the gym wall. Even with her eyes shut, she could sense the volleyballs zooming from one side of the room to the other. Skin slapped leather. The breeze of volleyballs and rushing bodies tickled her cheeks with the hairs that had slipped out of her ponytail.

"Heads up!"

Vivian's eyes opened in time to see the white mass bounce off the floor directly in front of her, just before it struck her in the forehead. Laughter rippled across the gymnasium.

"Bennett, are you okay?" Mr. Jackson jogged across the gym, his sneakers screeching against the lacquered floor.

Vivian squeezed her eyes against the embarrassment of her classmates' laughter. She had already twisted her ankle while going after a volleyball and wobbled off the court, while her peers gawked at her. Now a head shot while she iced her lame ankle. Could this gym class get any more humiliating?

Mr. Jackson knelt beside her as he eyed the scar that etched a trail above her eye. "Do you need to see the nurse? That was a pretty hard hit."

Vivian thought about it for a second. Honestly, she was fine, but it would get her away from the scrutinizing eyes of her too curious classmates.

"Look, why don't you cut out a little early. Take your time getting showered up and changed. There's no sense in you sitting here, listening to this pack of animals pounding volleyballs."

"Alright," she agreed. The pain from her ankle shot through her leg, causing her to wince as she stood up.

"Clare, why don't you make sure Vivian gets to the locker room okay."

"Sure, Mr. Jackson." Vivian allowed Clare to pull her to her feet.

"I could walk her down, Mr. J," Grant offered from somewhere in the crowd of students standing around the gymnasium.

"If it's all the same to you, Grant, I'd rather keep boys out of the girls' locker room."

Giggles scattered across the gym.

"I wasn't actually going to walk *in* with her."

Vivian scanned the gym and found Grant smiling sympathetically at her. One of Hailey's friends peered up from her cell phone at Grant as she pressed at the screen. Vivian grinned back at Grant before limping beside Clare through the double doors into the hallway.

The muggy air of the gymnasium, tainted with the smell of sweaty shorts, was a stark contrast to the chilly air of the corridor. Vivian rubbed the goosebumps that speckled her arms brought on by the sudden coolness.

"I'm sorry you got nailed in the head," Clare offered kindly, eyeing the scar above Vivian's eye.

"Thanks. I'll be fine," Vivian replied, pushing the heavy, wooden door of the locker room with her shoulder as she glanced back at Clare. "I can probably manage from here."

Vivian winced as a sharp pain shot up her leg. She

pressed her back against the door as she adjusted her weight off her injured ankle.

"Let me help you get to the bench in front of your locker."

"We can take it from here." Hailey's voice echoed off the brick walls off the hallway. Three of Hailey's friends pushed past Clare, grabbing Vivian by her arms as they dragged her into the locker room.

"You can go back to class, now. And no one needs to know we're in here," Hailey spat, sneering as she pushed the door shut behind them. A puff of black smoke swirled around her ankles as a shadow figure began to take shape, crawling up her legs like an oversized spider.

The girls dragged Vivian toward a row of lockers. Her feet slid across the concrete before her body was slammed into the metal doors. A padlock dug between her shoulder blades, as Hailey's breath warmed her face.

"I told you to stay away from my boyfriend."

Vivian tried to pull her arms out of the clutches of the two girls who stood beside her, pressing her arms against the cold metal of the lockers behind her. Their fingers dug into her flesh as they tried to control her squirming body. A third girl stood watch at the locker room door. Hailey placed her palm firmly on Vivian's forehead before slamming her head against the locker she was pinned against. Vivian choked back a moan.

"What's the matter? Got a headache?" Hailey mocked with a sneer.

The shadow figure had grown into a creature twice the size of Hailey. What had once been a thin wisp of smoke had transformed into what appeared to be a very tall man with bulging shoulders, a thick neck, and a smooth, hairless head. Red eyes, set deeply in an angular face, glowered down at Vivian. Raspy breaths hissed past leathery lips which dripped trails of mucus with each exhalation.

Vivian glared back, unwilling to let the moan rising into her throat slip past her lips.

"It's not too bad. Thanks for your concern."

The shadow cocked its head sharply to one side, a low growl rumbling through clenched teeth.

Glancing at the girls on either side of her, still clutching her arms, Vivian said, "It's so nice of you and your friends to help me into the locker room."

Hailey put both hands on Vivian's face and slammed her head against the locker again. A hollow thud echoed through the room. With the sound ringing in her ears, Vivian kicked at Hailey, as she struggled against the grasp of the two girls who pinned her arms beside her.

"Orphans shouldn't be so mouthy." Hailey pressed a finger into the thickened scar that puffed above Vivian's eye.

Although Vivian's eyes were open, Hailey's angry face blurred as everything around her went black. The groan Vivian had tried to hold back escaped. She heard the girls laugh as her body slumped forward, her arms still pressed against the steel gray lockers behind her. The weight of her body pulled awkwardly at the ligaments and tendons in her joints, making her shoulders ache.

Hailey used a fistful of Vivian's hair to pull her head up. As the metal locker rattled against the weight of her head, Vivian's vision returned.

"Don't go to homecoming with Grant Saturday, or you'll pay." Hailey's nose nearly touched Vivian's face as her breath moistened Vivian's cheeks.

The sound of an object cutting through the air made Hailey look behind her. Her body lurched forward as the rush of air ended with a thwack against her shoulder.

"Let her go or I'll bust this broom handle over your head." The voice was familiar, but Vivian struggled to place it. The room seemed to spin as she squinted to see through her dizziness. Hailey's friends dropped her arms as they hurried to Hailey.

"Hailey, are you okay?" The girl standing watch rushed to the group.

"I'm fine," Hailey grumbled, rubbing her shoulder. "You didn't have to hit me, you freak!" Her voice was shrill and teetered on hysterics.

Hailey's shadow figure had shrunk slightly and peered almost cautiously around her shoulder. It seethed quietly and scratched at the air.

"When I see a bunch of preppy snobs beating on my friend, I'm going to swing first and ask questions later." Vivian recognized Jen's voice as she snapped back boldly.

"Chill, psycho! We were just having a friendly chat with Vivian," one of the girls said with a glare.

"And I suppose that was a group hug I saw?" Jen narrowed her eyes at the girl.

"Mind your own business!" Hailey snapped.

"Yeah, there's four of us and only one of you. You better back off!" The tallest of the girls moved closer to Jen, her fists clenched at her sides.

The locker room door squeaked open, and Mrs. Hammer walked in briskly.

"What's going on here, girls?" She glanced from Jen to Vivian and then at Hailey and her crew.

"Nothing, Mrs. Hammer. We were just talking," Hailey said, her voice dripping with sweetness.

"Vivian, is that true?" Mrs. Hammer looked skeptical.

"Yes. We were just talking. I'm fine."

"Jennifer?" Mrs. Hammer looked at the broom she held in her hand.

"It was a heated conversation," Vivian offered. "But it's done now."

"We do not tolerate violence in this school, girls. If I hear of any fighting, you will be expelled." Mrs. Hammer directed her gaze at Hailey and her friends.

"Of course, Mrs. Hammer, we would never be violent," Hailey protested.

"I assume you girls should be in a class somewhere. I suggest you get there right now."

"Yes, ma'am," Hailey replied as she and her posse hurried toward the door.

Mrs. Hammer put a hand on Jen's back, and gently placed her other hand around the broom handle. "I assume you no longer need this," she said softly, as she took the broom from Jen's hands.

"Vivian, if anyone is giving you a hard time, please tell me or one of your other teachers. You don't need to tolerate anyone harassing you."

"Thank you. I will." Vivian smiled weakly.

"Jennifer, if possible, next time find an adult to help. We don't want anyone resorting to violence."

Jen pushed the blue tips of her bangs away from her eyes. "Okay."

Mrs. Hammer left the room as quickly as she had entered, the broom tucked under her arm. As she plopped on the bench, Vivian looked up gratefully at Jen. Something was different about her, but Vivian wasn't sure exactly what it was.

"Thanks, Jen. I don't know what you were doing in here, but I'm so glad you were around."

"Sometimes I skip eighth period and hide out in one of the bathrooms. I came down here to get my iPod charger out of my gym bag. I was sitting in the corner listening to Green Day when I heard that weasel Hailey giving you a hard time."

Vivian propped her elbows on her knees and let her head drop into her hands. Having her head hammered against the metal lockers had created an almost unbearable throbbing behind her scar.

"Vivian, are you alright?" Clare rushed through the gym doors with Emily on her heels. "I ran to Mrs. Hammer's office as fast as I could. I'm sorry I left you, Vivian. I wasn't sure what to do."

Vivian mumbled into her palms, "It's alright, Clare. I just..." The pounding in her head made her feel nauseated. "I don't...feel...well." She struggled to get the words out as she breathed deeply, trying to suppress the bile rising in her throat.

"Let's get her to the nurse," Emily suggested.

Jen and Clare pushed their shoulders under Vivian's arms, lifting her from the bench. Emily held the door as they led her into the main corridor. Vivian stumbled through the hallway while the two girls shouldered her weight, nearly carrying her to the main office. She squeezed her eyes shut to keep the walls from spinning around her.

When they reached the health office, the girls lowered Vivian onto the sea-foam-green cushion of the bed reserved for students who had vomited in class or were trying to ditch out on a test they had forgotten to study for. She rested her head on the plastic covered pillow and opened her eyes enough to glance at the white walls illuminated by the harsh fluorescent light humming overhead—the carcasses of dead bugs dotted its cover. The nurse bustled around the room and returned to Vivian's side with a large pill and a small paper cup, just big enough for a large gulp of water.

Despite how much she hated their effects, Vivian knew she needed one of her painkillers.

"Thanks, guys," she said after choking down the horse pill.

"Dude, that's like the biggest pill I've ever seen!" Jen exclaimed, as the three girls stood beside the bed looking down at Vivian.

"Guaranteed to dull the pain," Vivian replied. "I hate them."

The final bell rang, indicating the school day was over. The hallway outside the health office erupted with voices and the sounds of feet pounding toward the front doors, charging to freedom.

"Girls, you can go now. I've called Vivian's father to come pick her up." Nurse Pam smiled and shooed the trio toward the door.

Clare and Emily chirped goodbye as they were swallowed by the rush of bodies. Jen paused in the doorway and looked back at Vivian. Suddenly, Vivian realized what was different about Jen. She was alone. The shadow she had seen clinging to Jen's shoulder every day for the past few weeks was gone.

"Thanks again, Jen." Vivian smiled from her perch on the pleather bed.

"Thanks for giving me an excuse to whack Hailey." She beamed back. "I've been dreaming about doing that since first grade—literally."

Both girls giggled before Jen disappeared into the crowd.

Vivian rested on the bed, relaxing limb by limb as her medication took effect. A slight grin turned up the corners of her lips as she thought about Jen walking away alone. No shadow on her back harassing her. Just Jen in her dark clothes and heavy makeup, looking every bit as dark as she had the day before, but Vivian knew that she was a little lighter, a little more confident—maybe even a little happier.

Vivian smiled to herself as she rested her head on the paper-covered pillow.

"Well, at least you look like you're feeling alright." Grant's voice made her smile widen. "I heard Hailey came after you in the locker room." He looked down at his feet. "I'm so sorry, Vivian."

Vivian sat up and reached for Grant's hand. He was already wearing his football practice gear. The white fabric of his pants stretched tight against the firm muscles in his legs, which were just inches from her face. She tried to avoid looking at the firmness of his backside and she carried her eyes up to meet his gaze. "I'm okay."

Grant sat down on the edge of the small bed, returning her firm grasp on his hand. His thigh touching the side of her own made her heart jump inside her chest.

"She does this, every time we break up."

"She's done this before?"

"She just goes crazy. And then I feel horrible and we end up getting back together, but not this time. I'm done."

Vivian watched his brow furrow in determination, his jaw clenched. He looked up at the clock before locking eyes with Vivian.

"I have to go. I can't be late to practice or coach will make me run laps." He leaned in quickly and kissed her cheek. "I'm glad you're okay. You know, you're tougher than you look."

Vivian was sure her cheeks had turned red hot from the heat of his lips. "I'm going to take that as a compliment."

Grant stood and hurried to the door. He paused to smile back at Vivian, before disappearing into the crowd of students rushing through the hallway, leaving Vivian with her thoughts.

"Young love." Vivian had almost forgotten there was anyone else in the room. "You should probably lie back down. I'm sure that little kiss didn't do anything to ease your dizziness." Nurse Pam smiled.

Vivian's cheek flushed crimson before she let her head rest back on the pillow. She closed her eyes and relived the touch of Grant's lips in her mind.

CHAPTER SEVENTEEN

THE SCHOOL NURSE LEFT A FEW minutes after the bell rang, leaving Vivian alone with a heavy dose of painkillers coursing through her body. As the clock ticked the minutes away, Vivian laid on the bed, waiting for her father to pick her up. By the time she realized she had left her purse in her P.E. locker, the pain in her head and ankle had completely disappeared.

She peered into the main office. Ms. Miller, the school's secretary, sat at her desk typing on her keyboard.

"I left my purse in the locker room. Would you let my dad know I went to get it, if he comes before I get back?"

"Sure," Ms. Miller replied without looking away from her computer screen.

Like a feather, Vivian floated through the halls. Her body was nearly void of all feeling as the medication which had erased her pain had also deadened every nerve within her skin. Her legs were wet noodles as she wobbled toward the locker room, wondering if she looked as strange as she felt.

Using the weight of her body, she heaved the door open and drifted toward her locker. The padlock fumbled clumsily in her hands.

"Shoot," she grumbled as she passed the numbers she wanted to stop at. Her fingers refused to listen to her brain fast enough.

"Stupid pills," she mumbled, twisting the combination into the numbered wheel for the fourth time. When the lock released, she grabbed her purse from the metal hook inside.

As the metal door of the locker slammed shut, the overhead lights turned off, leaving Vivian in complete darkness. Frozen in surprise, her eyes widened, as they tried to adjust to the sudden blackness of her surroundings. A sliver of light trickled through a row of small windows located near the ceiling on the far wall of the room, several rows of lockers away.

"I'm in here," she called out, hoping whoever had switched off the lights might flip them back on. Her words echoed in the hollowness of the empty room. There was no response. No sudden burst of light—only dark and silence.

As her eyes adjusted to the murkiness of her surroundings, she edged around the wooden benches between the rows of lockers. Her breath came in rapid bursts, her heart pounding in her chest. Using her hands, she felt her way around one row of lockers.

There are two more rows of lockers, she thought. *Then the door will be to the right.* She moved slowly but steadily across the concrete floor.

"Vivian," Thane's voice spoke urgently through the blackness. *"Someone else is in here. They're near the door."* His words tumbled quickly into her ears.

Vivian stood very still and held her breath—listening to the silence. Only it was not completely silent. Raspy breaths whispered from somewhere in the darkness. Her eyes widened, as she searched for someone obscured by the deep black of the room.

"Who's there?" Her voice trembled as she called out.

Three slow, heavy footsteps were the only reply she heard. The raspy breathing seemed to fill the room around her from every direction. Already battling the numbing effects of her medication, her head began to spin and her legs trembled beneath the weight of her fear.

Two more steps moved toward her. She inched backwards, deeper into the locker room.

"My dad's waiting for me," she shouted. "He knows I'm in here!" It was only a partial lie. He might still be driving to the school for all she knew.

Four slow steps.

For a moment, the adrenaline from fear overpowered the medication that deadened her nerves, and Vivian turned around, hurrying away from the sound. Falling over a bench, she cracked her elbow on the concrete floor. The footsteps rushed toward her as she struggled to her feet. Pivoting on her heels she prepared to run down the length of the row of lockers she stood in, but before she could move, hands grabbed her hair from behind. Her body was jerked backward as her unseen assailant dragged her toward the showers.

Her screams echoed through the room as she slapped at the hands gripping her hair.

The explosive sound of lockers being hit, one after another, drowned out Vivian's screams. The pounding started toward the far end of the row she was being dragged down and hurried toward her.

Bang. Bang. Bang.

The startled attacker released her, as the lockers directly beside them began to rattle against an invisible fist.

"Run, Vivian! Run for the door!" Thane's voice called over the crash of the metal doors as his ghostly hands pounded on them.

Vivian put one hand in front of her as she hurried through the darkness. She let her other hand run along the lockers beside her, keeping her body close to them, to avoid the wooden benches. As she rounded the corner and entered the last row of lockers, she began to sprint toward the thin stream of light peeking under the door.

Thane continued to pound the lockers around her attacker, slowing them down with the confusion, but not completely ceasing their pursuit. Vivian could hear footsteps pound against the concrete as they rushed toward her.

She pulled the door open with a sudden surge of adrenaline-induced strength and burst into the hallway. Sprinting, she never looked back to see if anyone followed her. As she rushed around the corner of the gym wing into the commons area, she crashed into someone, knocking them onto the floor in front of her. Tripping over their body, she slid across the tiles on her stomach.

She heard her father moan. "Vivian?"

The combination of the painkillers and the exhaustion from the terror she felt made her too weak to stand. She lay on the floor, crying as her father knelt beside her and lifted her into his arms.

"What is it, Vivian?"

"Someone attacked me in the locker room!"

"I know. When the nurse called, she told me there had been an altercation before you were brought to her office."

"No, Dad, just now! I went to get my purse from my locker and someone was there. They turned off the lights and..." her voice cracked as sobs shook her body.

She looked over her father's shoulder toward the corridor she had just run through. Thane stood in the doorway. His shoulders slumped as he looked from Vivian then toward the locker room behind him. His image began to flicker, fading in and out.

"Thane..." Vivian moaned as the room around her spun.

James looked toward the doorway. "Is he here, Vivian? What do you see?"

"He looks...so...tired." She could barely get the words

across her lips. The drowsiness caused by her painkillers was beginning to take over.

"They had me," she whispered as she faded in and out of consciousness. "But Thane...saved me."

Her body hung limply in her father's arms as the world went black.

THEY STOOD IN FRONT of the mirror, glaring spitefully at their own reflection. The irises of their eyes were like black holes to their equally dark soul.

"You're so stupid!"

Breath fogged the reflection.

"You had her, and you let her get away! Stupid. Stupid. Stupid."

Fingernails scratch at their forearms. Their breath pulsed in jagged spurts as they dug red trails across their flesh.

"How did she make the lockers slam around her?"

Confusion twisted through their thoughts.

"Could she be more powerful than me? There's more to her than I can see—much more."

CHAPTER EIGHTEEN

THE CREAK OF A FLOORBOARD PULLED Vivian out of the heavy slumber her medication had induced. She opened her eyes too quickly and was welcomed to consciousness by dizzying motion in her head. After clenching her eyes shut, she slowly opened one—then the other.

A door creaked and clicked shut. The sound seemed to come from inside her room—her closet, maybe. Slowly lifting her head, she peered toward her closet. Rebecca placed a laundry basket on the floor, before sitting down beside James on the chaise lounge. His face was buried in his hands, his elbows propped on his knees. Rebecca put her arm around his shoulder and kissed the top of his head. Thane stood beside them, looking down at them quietly. The starlit sky framed by the window behind them created an almost heavenly glow.

"What if someone is trying to hurt her, Rebecca?"

"They searched the locker room. There was no one there, James."

"She was terrified. You should have seen her."

"Maybe her mediation, coupled with the stress of so many changes in the past two months, caused her to see things."

"She said Thane saved her. She sees things, Rebecca. Spirits. She always has."

"How is that possible, James? I don't understand."

"He did save me, Dad." Vivian's voice was weak and gravely. "Somehow he banged on the lockers when whoever attacked me was dragging me toward the showers. I didn't know spirits could do that—hit things like that. But he did."

Vivian's father rushed to her bed and sat beside her. "He *was* there?"

"Yes. He looked so tired when I saw him in the hallway after I ran into you. Like banging on the lockers had drained him of all his strength." Thane sat on the other side of Vivian and watched their father as he spoke.

"I didn't know I could do that either. But when I saw them hurting you, I somehow found this strength I didn't know I had. I punched the locker because I was so mad I couldn't help you. When it made a noise, I almost couldn't believe I'd done it."

"Did it hurt you?" Vivian asked aloud.

"It just made me so tired. I knew I should go back 'to the light' or whatever you want to call it, but I wouldn't leave, until I knew you were safe."

"Is he here, right now?" her father asked anxiously.

"Yes."

A tear slid from the corner of James's eye as he bit his lip. He looked down solemnly. "He must hate me."

"I don't," Thane replied. *"Tell him, Viv. Tell him I don't hate him."*

"Well, you should hate him!" Vivian clenched her teeth.

"What?" her father asked.

"Please tell him. I can't do it myself." Thane looked at her with pleading eyes.

"Fine!" She took several deep breaths through pursed lips as her father studied her quietly. Blowing one more breath heavily through her nose she mumbled, "Thane says he doesn't hate you."

Her father put his hand to his mouth, holding back a sob as tears spilled down his cheeks.

"Tell him I love him."

Vivian bit her lip as she squeezed her eyes shut.

"Please, I've been trying to tell him since we got here, but he can't hear me like you can."

"Why would you want to tell him that?"

"Because I didn't get to say it when I was alive."

Vivian shook her head as she gazed at her brother. Perched beside her, he seemed so real—so much a part of her life. But he was gone. His body lay on a velvet bed closed inside a glossy, mahogany box—the same casket as their mother's, only smaller. Under the dirt. Under fresh sod. Under a small headstone etched with the date he was born and the date he died. Just a kid. Strangers would walk past his gravestone and say, "How sad," as they contemplated the ways he might have died so young.

James watched quietly while Vivian glared at the empty space on her bed. Her eyes became pools of tears.

"Please, Vivian."

"Thane wants you to know that he loves you. Don't ask me to say the same for myself," she muttered bitterly. "I won't."

James bit his quivering lip. "Thank you for telling me."

He stood slowly. He seemed to be aging faster each day. The skin under his eyes was dark and puffy. Gray hairs speckled the stubble on his face.

"I love him, too. I tell him every day."

"I hear you, Dad."

"He knows." Vivian twisted her hair as she stared at the bedspread covering her legs, the tears that had filled her eyes creating dark spots on the fabric.

Her father walked toward her bedroom door. With his hand on the knob, he turned to look at his daughter. Her jaw was set with a righteous anger that he might never break through. She glanced up at him.

"I love you, too, Vivian. I'm sorry I've let you down so much. You have every right to hate me, but I pray one day you won't anymore."

He disappeared through the door. A few seconds later, his bedroom door down the hallway clicked shut.

Rebecca picked up the laundry basket and stopped at Vivian's bedside.

"I hesitate to say anything about your relationship with your father, Vivian. And I know he has disappointed you very deeply," Rebecca said timidly, her brow furrowed as she seemed to be searching for the right words to say. "But I want you to know he did try to contact you all those months. I heard him argue with your mother on the phone, pleading with her to let him speak to you kids. I saw him write you and Thane letters, only to find them in the mailbox unopened with 'return to sender' written across the front of the envelope."

"That can't be true," Vivian replied instinctively, shaking her head. "My mother wouldn't do that."

"Love makes us do things that don't make a whole lot of sense sometimes. Your father would never come out and say it, but I think it was because of me," Rebecca said looking at the floor sadly.

Vivian stared at her stepmother, trying to process what she was telling her. The impulse to scream and possibly even slap her had been buffered by the sadness she saw in Rebecca's eyes. She had been nothing but nice to Vivian. She found it difficult to be upset with her stepmother, even as Rebecca was telling her that her mother might have been the reason for the estrangement from her father she had suffered through for so many months.

"I spoke to her once when she called, and she told me I had ruined everything. Maybe she had held onto some hope that she and your father might get back together one day. I'm not sure. I just know that when your father and I got married, she was so hurt."

Vivian did recall her mother seemed withdrawn for a few weeks after she told them their father had eloped. But it was difficult for her to believe her mother would shut him out of their lives completely because of her own jealousy.

"Your father loves you and Thane so much, Vivian. He will always regret not trying harder to see you. He's not a perfect person, but he's not a bad person either."

With the laundry basket balanced on one hip, Rebecca took Vivian's hand in her own and looked into her eyes.

"Just promise me you'll try to forgive him, Vivian—if not for him, for yourself."

Vivian searched her stepmother's eyes for any indication that she might be lying. She looked nothing but completely sincere.

"I'll try," Vivian promised.

"Thank you." Rebecca smiled warmly. "I've put a tray with soup and crackers on your nightstand. There's some ginger ale, too. James said your medication makes you nauseous. Ginger ale always helps my stomach feel better."

She set the basket of folded clothes on the edge of the bed, before bending down and hugging Vivian tightly. Vivian hugged back. Her ice-cold anger melted into her stepmother's embrace.

"We both love you, honey. We'll be down the hall in our room, if you need anything at all," she assured Vivian as she scooped up the basket and walked toward the door.

"Thank you."

Vivian stared at the ceiling after the door shut behind Rebecca. She was alone. Even Thane had disappeared. He had probably gone to be near their father.

Another wave of nausea coursed through her, as she considered what Rebecca said. It was almost too much to think about. Beads of sweat dotted her forehead. Kicking off her blankets, she sat up enough to reach the ginger ale on her nightstand. Her stomach settled as the dizziness she had felt when she'd first woken up began to go away.

Saltine crackers fanned a bowl of chicken noodle soup in the center of a bone-white plate. Vivian crushed a few of the crackers into the bowl and spooned a heap of warm noodles into her mouth. She ate until the bowl was clean, even scrapping the crumbs from the sides of the dish with her index finger.

As she stretched her arms above her head, Vivian swung her legs over the side of her bed. She looked through the window across the room and wondered how long she had been asleep. The clock on her nightstand read eight-thirty. She must have passed out at school. She had absolutely no memory of getting home.

The events of that afternoon seemed like a bad dream. She teetered between believing she had been attacked, and considering the possibility that Rebecca might have been right about her having had a horrible reaction to her medication. But the tenderness on the back of her head where her hair had been used to drag her struggling body across the locker room assured her it had not been a dream.

Someone attacked me, but who?

Vivian could not imagine anyone wanting to really hurt her. Even Hailey and her friends did not seem like the types who would want to cause her actual harm. Harass and intimidate, yes. But actually hurt? She just could not believe it.

Unsure of how her body would respond to any sudden motion, Vivian slowly rose to her feet. She was prepared for another round of dizziness and nausea, but was relieved to find herself feeling relatively steady. The soup and ginger ale had washed away any remnants of her grogginess.

She moved steadily across the room and, stopping in front of the window, gazed over the canopy of trees below. It was a breezeless evening. The few stubborn leaves clinging to the nearly bare branches hung motionless. The twinkle of a million stars lit the sky as a full moon hung like a spotlight against the blackness of nightfall.

As Vivian scanned the trees below, she saw her. Sarah gazed toward the window, her torn night gown hanging loosely around her body. Her head tilted unnaturally toward one shoulder. Muddy tear-trails stained her cheeks.

Slowly, one arm rose. Sarah's outstretched finger pointed at Vivian, then motioned for her to come. Hesitantly, she turned and began to walk into the trees, looking over her shoulder to glance at Vivian every few steps.

The rational part of Vivian's brain screamed for her to stay put—begged her to yell for her dad and Rebecca. But something inside of her kept her silent. Her feet, independent of thought, moved her body toward the door. It was as if she were being pulled across the room by an unseen hand.

As she passed her nightstand, she reached into the drawer and retrieved the silver bracelet Sarah's spirit had left in her room a few days before. Her fist clutched tightly around it, as she hurried into the hallway.

She drifted through the house in a trancelike state until she stood in the backyard, steps away from the dense trees that butted the freshly trimmed grass. A wisp of pale blue skittered behind an evergreen bush as Vivian scanned the trunks and nearly naked branches of the trees and undergrowth.

"Sarah?" Vivian whispered into the still night. Her voice met an unnatural silence that chilled her from the inside. There were no chirping crickets, no toads croaking from the pond a few hundred yards through the thicket—just dead silence.

Vivian saw Sarah's frail form peer shyly from behind the evergreen. She put one finger to her lips as if warning Vivian that someone or something might be listening. Vivian nodded and carefully stepped into the trees, trying to move quickly while making as little noise as possible. She kept an eye on

Sarah, while maneuvering around the broken branches on the forest floor beneath her.

It wasn't until her foot caught on the twisted root of a nearby tree that she realized she had left the house barefoot, wearing only a thin t-shirt and cotton shorts. Though the air was still, the chill of the cool autumn temperature cut through the fabric like the blade of a razor.

She should have felt cold. The thistles and dried twigs that dug into her bare feet should have made her wince with pain. But she did not feel the cold or the branches digging into her soft flesh. She did not feel anything, beyond the urgent need to follow. It was as if she were separate from her body, as she was pulled toward something Sarah's spirit needed her to see.

As she emerged into a small clearing around the pond, she saw Sarah sitting under a willow tree, her knees drawn to her chest, torn bits of blue fabric hanging down her left calf. Vivian jogged across the space between them and breathlessly knelt in front of her.

"What is it, Sarah? What do you want to show me?"

Taking Vivian's hands, she pulled her closer until her mud streaked cheek pressed against Vivian's. Strands of Sarah's hair brushed against Vivian's ear, and the clumps of dried dirt matted in it pressed against Vivian's scalp. Bits of brown leaves tangled in Sarah's hair crunched loudly as she pressed as close as she could. The iciness of her skin caused Vivian to shiver.

"See through my eyes."

The dry hiss of her barely audible words blew into Vivian's ear as she suddenly found herself lying on her back on the cold, damp ground. No, not *on* the ground—*in* it. Within seconds, she realized she had been here once before—in her dream.

Dirt rained onto her body. Glancing down, she saw she wore the same blue nightgown she had just seen on Sarah. Her hands were freshly welted with deep purple contusions and splattered with flecks of drying blood. A fingernail had been ripped off of her middle finger, exposing the raw, pink flesh beneath. These hands had clawed and fought for life. It was a fight they had lost.

The heart pendant fastened to a thin, silver bracelet strung around her wrist, resting on the back of her bruised and bloodied hand.

More dirt pelted her face. Bits of soil slipped between her lips. It had the taste of pond water. A hand reached into the shallow grave and grabbed at the bracelet. The tug only lifted her arm away from her body, spraying dirt through the air. Her hand slapped against her stomach with a dull thud. A second tug broke the thin chain, releasing the bracelet from her wrist.

Vivian struggled to see through the layer of damp soil covering her face. The clumps of earth felt heavy against her lids. Through a blur of dirt, Vivian saw a figure leaning over her, studying her lifeless body.

Vivian could see it was a human form, but the details of the person were shrouded by a dark shadow that seemed to wrap itself like a thick blanket around the human, whose hands wielded the shovel. The figure was framed by the swaying drapes of the willow tree that shaded the shallow grave.

"*Vivian.*" Thane's voice urgently called her back to reality. "*Someone's coming!*"

Vivian found herself staring up at the same view of the willow tree she had seen in her vision. Now she lay on top of the ground rather than in it. Moonlight glistened off the slick leaves that were slow to change with the season.

"*Stay low, Vivian! Hide behind the bushes over there!*"

Vivian rolled onto her knees and crawled across the hard, cold ground. The smell of wet dirt hung in her nostrils as she crouched behind a thick evergreen bush, her body scrunched into a ball, her chin resting on the ground.

On the other side of the lone willow, a murky shape emerged through the wall of trees. The nearly full moon illuminated the figure as it moved fully into the clearing. Anna stood in the moonlight, holding a quilt over her arm, a lantern in one hand, and a book in the other. She spread the quilt out in the ground beneath the willow tree—the very spot Vivian had just been lying, reliving the burial of Sarah Christian's lifeless body—and set the lantern in one corner and the book beside it. Then she settled onto the quilt with her stomach on the ground, elbows propped up in front of her, feet crisscrossed in the air behind her.

As she flipped the book open, Anna froze, staring at the ground in front of her. She closed the book, and crawled across the blanket on her hands and knees. Straining her neck, Vivian peeked around the bush. She followed Anna's gaze toward the ground. In the moonlight, something glittered in the tufts of grass near the edge of Anna's quilt. Vivian clasped her hand over mouth as she stifled a gasp.

The bracelet. She had been holding it when she sat in that spot with Sarah's spirit. She must have dropped it.

Anna reached forward as a look of pure confusion etched her face. While she picked up the bracelet, she glanced around, peering in every direction into the trees surrounding her.

"Sarah?" she whispered into the trees. "Are you here?"

Vivian held her breath and didn't move. She was tempted to jump from her hiding place and tell Anna everything that had been happening, but she wasn't sure who she could trust. Although in her heart, she believed that Anna could be trusted, everything was too uncertain. At the very least, revealing her strange ability might terrify her new friend. She wasn't sure she should have told Grant, but it was too late to take her revelation back now.

Anna squinted into the trees.

"Sarah?"

A branch broke somewhere on the opposite side of the clearing from where Vivian hid. Anna's eyes widened in fear as she quickly gathered up her things and rushed through the trees, dragging the quilt along the ground as she ran.

Vivian remained frozen behind the bush, as she stared in the direction of the broken twig. Slowly, a form rustled through the underbrush, as a deer moved into the moonlight. Vivian sighed quietly with relief.

Then another branch broke from somewhere far away. The sound startled the deer, causing it to rush back into the trees. It could have been Anna running through the woods. It could have been another deer, but the sound created a sense of fear in Vivian that made her heart race.

Thane stood beside her, staring into the trees.

"It doesn't feel safe out here, Vivian. You need to get back to the house. Something's wrong."

"I know," she replied in a whisper. "I had the same feeling."

She rose cautiously from her hiding place and hurried toward the back door of the house. As she hustled up the porch steps, she paused and looked behind her with the unshakable feeling that someone was standing just beyond her sight, watching her. Quietly, she slipped into the house through the backdoor, latching the lock behind her.

As she hurried through the hallway toward the foyer, she paused at the basement door. Holding her breath, she turned the knob and pulled. It held firmly locked shut. She breathed a held breath out loudly and tiptoed the rest of the way through the house and back to her bedroom.

She moved her backpack off the chair near her closet and wedged the back of the chair under her bedroom doorknob.

"Just in case," she said before taking one last look out her window.

The moon lit the forest floor where it peeked through the leafless trees, their bare branches motionless in the still night.

There was no sign of Anna or Sarah or any other living thing in the trees beyond the yard, but Vivian still searched through the trees and brush for someone, or something. She could not shake the feeling that there was more than she could see.

THEY GAZED LONGINGLY AT her as she stood at the window.

Where had she been earlier when they had come to watch her? Her light had been on, but her room was still. Maybe she had been sleeping. For a moment, they thought they smelled her strawberry shampoo in the air around them, but they had not seen her among the trees.

They scratched at the bark on the trunk they hid behind, biting their lip until the metallic taste of blood dribbled onto their tongue.

Not much longer now. Somehow she had gotten away today, but tomorrow would be different. Tomorrow they would have her, just as they had planned.

CHAPTER NINETEEN

VIVIAN MANAGED TO SLIP INTO A RESTLESS sleep where her dreams were haunted by Sarah and Nancy. Images of their deaths clung to her mind, as she pulled herself into consciousness—away from the darkness of her dreams and into the darkness of her reality. A reality shrouded by shadows lurking in the corners of rooms. Watching. Waiting.

What the dark spirits waited for exactly, she wasn't sure. She only knew that they were there. She could sense their presence and their strength. A dark power she had never imagined could exist in this world, but in this house, the powers were strong. Stifling.

She sensed the darkness the moment she stepped through the front doors. And the spirits, both good and evil, had been drawn to her. Now they knew for certain she could see them, and she was sure they would not leave her alone until she did what needed to be done.

The heat from the sun beating through the bedroom window should have made Vivian hot under her blankets. Instead, she shivered as she glanced around the room wondering if the shadow figures were watching her at that moment. From the corner of her eye, she thought she saw a dark movement in a deep recess of her bedroom. She snapped her head toward it in time to see the trail of a shadow sliding up the corner of the wall.

As she rose from her bed, her heart raced. Her feet ached as she hurried toward the window. The cuts and scrapes she had gotten from running barefoot through the trees the night before had scabbed over. Her toenails were caked in dried mud.

Shielding her eyes from the sun, she peered into the trees. A shiver of fear raised the small hairs on the back of her neck. She glanced over her shoulder toward the wall where she had seen the moving shadow. Everything was still.

Just beyond the bare branches and spiny pines, Vivian felt sure, lay the body of Sarah Christian. Buried beneath a weeping willow. Beside a small pond. Her body likely nothing more than bones. Her flesh had certainly become earth as time and bugs did what they do to all things that lay dead in nature.

She pressed her forehead against the glass, hoping the extra fraction of an inch would improve her line of vision. It didn't work. Though the trees were nearly bare, the multitude of trunks rising toward the skyline obscured her view of the lonely willow tree which served as Sarah's grave stone.

It seemed odd to Vivian that she should care so much about helping someone she had never known in life. But Sarah's spirit seemed so tortured and desperate. Her life had barely begun, when someone had taken it from her.

Vivian wondered what Sarah wanted to do after high school. Had she planned to go to college? Did she dream of marrying a boyfriend? She had probably written his name a thousand times in her notebooks. Maybe she had even used his last name as her own, when she'd written her signature.

Sarah had been a girl like Vivian. Young and full of promise. Tortured by the things she couldn't change—like the death of her mother. Vivian imagined they would have been friends if she were still alive, just as she and Anna had become such fast friends—bound to one another by the sting of death.

Vivian abandoned the window and hurried toward the door.

She had to tell her father what she had seen. She had to find Sarah's body, so her spirit could rest. Somehow, she was certain doing that would bring peace to Nancy's spirit as well.

She rushed out of her room, leaving the door open.

Behind her, the shadows in the corners of the walls began to move. They swarmed from their hiding places like a disturbed bed of snakes and slithered across the ceiling and walls toward her. The air hissed as they slid into the hallway.

The hallway grew cold as they sucked the warmth from the air. A chilled puff of breath formed a tiny cloud in front of Vivian's lips as she watched the walls of the hallway crawling with darkness.

"Dad," she called out toward his bedroom.

Poking her head through the already opened door, she saw the bed was neatly made. The door to the bathroom stood opened.

Pivoting on the balls of her feet, she rushed to the stairs. Her eyes focused straight ahead, refusing to look up at the mass of shadows she knew prowled above her. When she reached the landing, she paused briefly and looked into the bedroom, which she was now sure was the place where Sarah had taken her final breath.

"Dad! Rebecca!" She nearly tripped on the steps as she hurried down them.

"In the kitchen," Rebecca replied.

Vivian skidded across the tiled floor of the kitchen, her body crashing into the table, toppling over her father's cup. He leapt from his seat as a small pool of coffee dribbled over the edge of the table onto his lap.

"Vivian!" her father exclaimed, reaching for her

shoulders to steady her body as she slipped again, trying to maneuver around the table. "What's going on?"

Vivian caught her breath and tried to calm herself before continuing. She wasn't sure how to tell her father what she was about to say, so she just said it.

"I know what happened to Sarah Christian! I saw her body being lowered out of her room through the dumbwaiter and..." The words tumbled past her lips in a frenzied rush. "She was murdered! I'm sure of it!"

Rebecca looked up from wiping the table.

"What? Vivian, she disappeared more than a year ago. How could you possibly see her body in the dumbwaiter?"

"I saw it in a vision!"

Vivian locked eyes with Rebecca, silently pleading with her to believe her.

Rebecca shook her head as she flashed a skeptical look at James.

"I don't understand." Rebecca regarded Vivian with concern, as she looked down toward her feet, which were caked in mud. "Why are you so dirty?"

Vivian let Rebecca's question hang in the air unanswered. She needed to make her father understand what happened to Sarah.

"I know it sounds crazy, but Sarah's spirit has been visiting me—trying to show me what happened to her. She did not run away. She was murdered! In the pink bedroom. Dad, you have to believe me!"

James pulled Vivian close to him and protectively wrapped his arms around her tightly.

"I believe you, Vivian."

Vivian leaned into his hug, so grateful he would listen. Gently, he eased her into a chair beside him.

"Tell us what she showed you," he directed firmly, his expression etched with unquestionable worry.

"I couldn't see *who* killed her, but I sensed it was

someone she knew. She left her bracelet on my floor the other morning. When I went to her bedroom, she showed me her body. It was stuffed in the dumbwaiter. She was dead. That was when you came in and found me in the pink bedroom at the top of the stairs."

"If she's dead, how could she give you a bracelet?" Rebecca frowned as she shook her head. "I just don't understand any of this."

"I don't understand it much either," Vivian confessed. "I didn't know they could move things or make noises like Thane did yesterday with the lockers. I don't understand how he manages to show up when I need him, like he did last night."

"Last night?" James eyes widened with concern. "What happened last night?"

Vivian told them about Sarah's spirit beckoning her into the woods. She told them about the vision of Sarah being buried under the willow tree. She paused for a long time before she went on.

"Anna was there last night." The words came out slowly, as if she was trying to make sense of them by speaking them out loud, more than she was trying to relay the information to her father or Rebecca.

"What? Why would she be out there in the middle of the night?"

"I don't know. She spread out a blanket on the exact spot where Sarah showed me she was buried and laid down to read, but then she saw the bracelet on the ground..."

"The one Sarah gave you," Rebecca interrupted, leaning forward as she listened intently.

"Yes. I know she was wearing it when she died, and her killer pulled it off her wrist as they buried her body," Vivian replied, relieved Rebecca finally seemed to believe her. "Anna picked it up. Then she started looking around and calling out Sarah's name."

James shook his head. "Like she thought she might be alive?"

"Maybe," Vivian agreed. "Or maybe like she knows Sarah's not alive, and she was half-expecting to see a ghost."

"Before we go any further with this, we need to make sure there *is* a body out there." James stood and grabbed a jacket off a coat hook, before hurrying out the backdoor.

Rebecca rushed to the door behind him. "James, wait! You shouldn't go alone!" She looked back at Vivian, her pupils dilated with fear. "This all scares me, Vivian. I think we should go with him."

Vivian hurried across the kitchen, threw on a pair of Rebecca's gardening sandals and a windbreaker. She grabbed a jacket from a hook and handed it to Rebecca.

"But you're still in your pajamas..." Rebecca began.

"I'm fine. Let's go!" Vivian exclaimed as she threw the backdoor open.

Slipping the jacket on, Rebecca hurried through the door behind her.

James emerged from the barn with a shovel under his arm. Long strides carried him toward the tree line. Vivian and Rebecca ran to his side. Together, they rushed through the trees toward the pond.

Vivian stopped beneath the overhang of yellowing willow leaves before shouting, "Right here! This is where she's buried!"

James ran to her side and plunged the steel blade into the ground, using the heel of his foot to push it deeper. A large mound of dirt heaped up beside him as he heaved it by the shovelfuls from the ground. Sweat dripped from his brows and chin, and soon he stood in a hole up to his chest.

"Do you think I should go deeper? Maybe I need to dig in a different spot."

Vivian stared into the immense crater her father had created, completely confused. Rebecca paced around them, peering into the trees, then into the hole, then back into the trees.

"I don't understand. She has to be there. I saw her lying *right* there, staring up at that tree." Vivian pointed toward the willow as her voice began to rise. "I saw her! She led me to this exact spot."

"Maybe she was confused. I mean, maybe spirits get confused about stuff like that," Rebecca offered. Vivian felt a sense of comfort knowing that now both Rebecca and her father believed her.

"No. She's here. She has to be."

"Mr. Bennett?"

Rebecca jumped when Raymond's voice boomed out of the trees behind her.

"I'm sorry, ma'am. I didn't mean to startle you."

"Oh, that's okay, Raymond. I just...didn't know you were there," she stuttered.

Raymond walked briskly toward the hole in which James stood, the blade of the shovel submerged in the soil.

"What are ya all doing here?"

Raymond looked from James to Rebecca, then to Vivian.

"We're looking for Sarah," Vivian replied firmly.

"We have reason to believe that Sarah Christian did not run away, as people have said. We've been informed she might have been murdered, and her body buried on the property."

Raymond peered into the hole as if expecting to see part of a body poking through the earth. "Let me help you dig. Anna," he called over his shoulder. "Run to the shed and get a shovel."

"Sure," she called back from somewhere through the trees.

"We were working on clearing the walking trail, but this seems more important, Mr. Bennett."

"Thank you, Raymond. I'd welcome your help."

The two men dug down and around the hole James had created. Sweat soaked through their clothes, despite the chilly temperatures. Streaks of dirt smeared their cheeks as they wiped the drips of perspiration from their brows.

James hoisted himself out of the hole, then reached in to help Raymond out. Rebecca, Vivian, and Anna stood beside them looking down into the crater.

It was empty. Void. There was absolutely nothing there. Not even a bone from a squirrel or long forgotten bird.

Vivian twisted her hair.

"I'm sorry, Dad. I thought...I don't know. I just..."

James put his arm around her shoulder, his sweat moistening the jacket she wore. "I know, Vivian. It's okay."

"I found Sarah's bracelet here last night," Anna said, confusion filled her eyes. "I must have dropped it when I ran along the trail, but it doesn't seem to be there anymore."

"What were you doing out here at night?" Raymond asked, with obvious concern.

"Sarah and I used to sneak out of our rooms at night and meet here. This was her favorite spot, under this tree, looking out at the pond." She looked at her father apologetically. "Sometimes, when I can't sleep, I still come here and read, or just think. But last night I found the bracelet under the tree, and I got scared."

"It's not safe to do such things, Anna," Raymond scolded. "Not with Nancy's murder and then Sarah going missing.

Anna looked at her feet.

Vivian was overwhelmed by the realization that her vision had been wrong. "I'm so sorry," her voice cracked, and she began to sob.

James put both hands on her shoulders and looked into her eyes. "It's okay, Vivian. No one is upset with you."

Rebecca took Vivian's hand. "Let's get some hot tea. Thank you for your help, Raymond."

"Yes, ma'am." He nodded, then looked at Anna sternly.

"We'll talk about you coming out here at night later. Back to that trail."

"Yes, sir." Turning to Vivian she asked, "Are you going to be okay?"

"Yeah, I'm alright. I'm just tired."

"Well, maybe you'd better get a nap in before tonight."

Vivian shook her head, "Tonight?"

"Homecoming? Your big date with Grant!"

In the confusion of the morning, Vivian had forgotten all about the homecoming dance.

"I'll come over around four and we can do our hair and makeup together like we planned. If you're still up to it."

"Of course she is," Rebecca replied. "We'll get some lunch, definitely a warm bath. She'll be ready. You just come on up to the house at four."

Rebecca and James formed a physical shield around Vivian. Rebecca kept her hand protectively grasped around Vivian's as James cradled Vivian's arm in the crook of his own, the shovel gripped in his free hand.

"I'm sorry. I don't understand." Vivian watched dead leaves and twigs as they crunched beneath her feet.

"Honey, you have been through so much," Rebecca said, squeezing Vivian's hand. "We love you and we're here for you, no matter what."

As they stood at the bottom of the porch steps, Vivian looked up shyly at her father. "It all seemed so real last night."

"Vivian, whatever's going on, we will figure it out."

"I'm just sorry I made you dig for hours and there was nothing there."

"You don't need to be sorry at all. If you tell me tomorrow that Sarah's body is buried in the front yard, I'll dig that up, too."

He grinned.

Vivian smiled back.

They walked up the short row of steps on the backside of

the wraparound porch, Vivian's arm still cradled in her father's.

Behind them, somewhere in the woodland, dried leaves and sprigs crunched lightly. Before following her father and stepmother into the house, Vivian glanced toward the faint sound.

Raymond Lowry leaned against a rake, as he watched the Bennett family cross the porch toward the door. When Vivian looked back at him, he quickly looked away and busied himself with scraping the metal teeth against the thick underbrush on the forest floor.

THEY WERE NOT HAPPY to see them digging under the tree, but they knew there was nothing there for them to find. Sarah was not there anymore. They had found a better place for her.

In the end, all that digging wouldn't matter.

They were still confused about finding Sarah's bracelet on the trail. However, it had gotten there didn't matter. They had returned it to where it belonged.

"Tonight, Vivian. Tonight, you will be the one they're looking for." They stifled the giggles that shook their shoulders, as they watched Vivian disappear into the back of the house.

CHAPTER TWENTY

VIVIAN SAT ON HER BED, HER wet hair pulled up in a towel wrapped around the top of her head. She fanned her toes apart with the pink, foam toe separator Rebecca had given her, before shaking the bottle of pink polish. The warm bath had helped her relax a bit, but her mind was still swimming with confusion over the events of the last twenty-four hours.

She replayed the night before, following the spirit of Sarah into the trees. What had she missed? Why would Sarah take her to that spot, if it was not where her body was?

A gentle tapping at her door brought her back the present.

"Come in," Vivian called out, assuming it would be Rebecca wanting to dote on her some more.

"It's me," Grant's voice said with uncertainty as he cracked the door open and peeked into the room. "Are you sure you're up for visitors?"

"Sure, of course," she said, trying to sound casual.

Grant smiled as he eyed the bundle on top of her head. Vivian felt her cheeks flush as she pulled the towel off in a panic. Running her fingers through her hair, she mumbled,

"Forgot that was on there."

"I think turbans are sexy."

Vivian laughed.

Grant sat on the bed beside her. He took the bottle of polish from her, shook it gently, and twisted off the cap, wiping the excess polish off on the rim.

"May I?" he asked, motioning toward her fanned out toes.

"You think turbans are sexy, and you like painting toenails. You're not like most boys I know."

He looked up from applying polish to her big toe. "You're not like most girls I know," he replied. He returned to painting. "I'm an only child, and I think my mom secretly wanted a girl, so she taught me how to paint her nails." He paused. "It's one of the things I would always do to try to cheer her up, after my dad was mean to her." His voice became quiet on the last couple words.

Vivian wasn't quite sure how to respond to Grant's reference to his father's abuse, so she just watched him silently as he focused on applying the polish to her toenails. He seemed content with the quiet as he worked, dipping the brush into the bottle, wiping the excess on the rim, and flawlessly sweeping the polishing over her nails. He twisted the top on the bottle when he was finished and placed it on her nightstand before gazing into Vivian's eyes thoughtfully.

"They look perfect," she said, admiring his precise paint job.

"*You* look perfect," he replied, still gazing at her eyes.

She blushed, returning his gaze. Silence hung between them for a few moments before he reached out and took her hand in his own.

"Anna told me what happened this morning," he finally said, "and yesterday at the school. Are you okay?"

"I'm fine," she replied quickly. His gentle gaze softened her resolve to be strong. "I mean, I'm mostly fine. Honestly,

Grant, I'm a little scared."

He squeezed her hand gently.

"There's something bad here. You know what you saw yesterday by the football field..."

"I know I saw something, but I don't know what," he said quietly.

"I'm not sure what it is exactly either, but I know it's something evil. And that same evil is all over this house. It seems to follow me."

"Is that why you went through the tunnel in the basement?" he asked.

"Partially. The darkness, like what you saw at the football field, was down there with me, but Sarah led me there. She wanted me to find the tunnel."

"Sarah? But that means..." he stopped, unable to finish the sentence.

"...she's dead," Vivian whispered. She watched Grant's face drain of all color. "And she needs my help. Only, I'm not sure how I can help her."

Tears welled up in Grant's eyes. "It was easier to think she had just run away, but I think I always knew she would never do that. Not without telling me, anyway."

"You two were close?" Vivian asked.

"We grew up together. My mom has been bringing me with her to work here as long as I can remember." A tear dropped onto the back of his hand, which still held Vivian's tightly. "When Sarah's mom died, she was so sad. She needed someone to talk to, and I was here so much..." he trailed off.

A mass of white began to form behind Grant.

"I knew it was wrong to be so close with her, because I had a girlfriend, and I wanted to break it off with Hailey, but she always made it so hard. And after how mean she was to Nancy when I started dating her, I was afraid of how they'd treat Sarah if anyone knew we liked each other."

The mass slowly took the shape of Sarah Christian. Her

transparent wisp of a hand reached out and gently touched Grant's shoulder. Grant shivered, as if chilled by the touch he was otherwise unaware of.

A black shadow seeped across the bedroom floor from the corner, like a slow-moving fog. Sarah's image turned to see the shadow rolling toward her, before flickering and vanishing as quickly as she had appeared. The shadow retreated back into the corners of the room.

Vivian, startled by the sudden display of spiritual energy, squeezed Grant's hand.

"I don't think it's safe for us to talk here," she whispered.

Grant looked around nervously. "Is that thing we saw at the football field here?" he asked, fear choking his words slightly as he spoke.

She nodded solemnly as she rose up from the bed, Grant's hand still firmly holding her own. They walked into the hallway and toward the stairs, pausing at the top, both glancing nervously into Sarah's bedroom. Shadows moved beyond the door just enough to cause the sunlight that shown through the pink curtains to seem alive beyond the threshold.

Vivian looked at Grant, wondering if he was able to see what she was seeing. His eyes widened as he looked into the room and, without looking away from the dizzying motion of the darkness moving around the room, he whispered, "What is that?" Vivian pulled him down the stairs, as he still looked back toward the room. They crossed the foyer. Her father glanced up from a magazine he was reading on the couch in the sitting room.

"We're just going outside," Vivian offered, before half-dragging Grant through the front door. They continued down the front steps and across the paved, circular drive, before dropping onto the grass in the tree-circled front yard, both facing the looming home.

"What was that?" Grant finally asked, breaking the unnerving silence.

"You saw it," Vivian said, eyeing him curiously. "No one else has ever seen it." She paused, staring back at the house. Even in the daylight, the sight of it made her shiver in fear. "I don't know what it is, but I know it's evil. And I'm pretty sure it has trapped Sarah's spirit here."

"Can we help her?" he asked looking directly into Vivian's eyes.

Vivian returned his gaze, suddenly shocked by the frank conversation they were having about spirits and shadows and seeing things that didn't make sense. It was like a weight had been lifted off her shoulders, even though she still faced the same terrifying reality now, that she had faced before. The difference was, she was no longer facing it alone. Somehow that truth gave her strength.

"I'm going to help her," she replied with determination.

"We're going to help her," Grant replied wrapping an arm protectively around her shoulder. She let her head rest against his solid shoulder. He gently kissed her forehead as a breeze picked up a few leaves from the grass near them and scattered them gently into the air.

For the first time since her mother and brother's deaths, she didn't feel alone.

CHAPTER TWENTY-ONE

"JUST ONE MORE SQUIRT, VIV." ANNA pointed the nozzle at Vivian's head and sprayed.

A cloud of hairspray lingered in the air. Vivian coughed as she accidentally breathed some of the fumes into her lungs.

"I'm pretty sure that was more than a squirt."

"Well, we don't want any curls falling out before Grant sees you, because you...look...perfect!" Anna paused dramatically before holding a hand mirror in front of Vivian.

"Oh, wow! How did you do that?"

Vivian glowed as she smiled into the mirror, then twisted her head so she could use the hand mirror to reflect the image of the back of her hair into the vanity behind her.

"My hair has *never* been so curly! Do you think it'll stay?"

Anna held up the can of hairspray. "Should we add an extra layer just to be safe?"

"No thanks. Lay off the trigger, shooter."

Anna smiled as she hesitantly put the can of extra-strong-hold hairspray down amid the tubes of lipstick and trays of shadows and blushes spread out on the vanity.

"Now I feel bad. I mean, I'm pretty sure you curled each

individual strand of my hair."

"I think I did."

"I flat ironed yours and put a bobby pin in it."

"It's a rhinestone bobby pin. What more does a girl need? Besides, my makeup looks so cool. I still cannot figure out how you got these lashes on straight."

"Once every couple of months, my mom would make me put lashes on her before she went out for girl's night. I've been doing it since I was seven."

"You're a pro!" Anna replied, smiling sympathetically. Her light brown hair seemed to glimmer in the lamp light. It cascaded down her back, over her thin, white shrug, and onto her sparkling emerald cocktail dress.

"If you told me then it would come in handy one day, I would have never believed you. But check us out. I'd say it's a skill worth having."

They gazed silently into the vanity mirror from their own reflection, then to each other's.

"Are you doing okay? I mean, after everything that happened yesterday...and then this morning?" Anna made eye contact with Vivian's reflection in the mirror.

Vivian turned to look at her face to face. Searching Anna's eyes, she wondered if she could trust her friend with the truth. "I'm okay," she began. "It's just..."

A gentle knock made them turn away from their images. The door cracked open just far enough for Rebecca to peak her head into the room.

"Oh my goodness! Look at the two of you!" she gushed as she hurried into the room, a camera clutched in one hand. "Can I get a few candid shots, before we head downstairs?"

"Sure," Vivian replied.

Anna looked at Vivian thoughtfully.

"I really am okay," Vivian said. She was certain she could trust Anna, or at least she was almost certain, but something made her hold back. An instinct, maybe. Or just the fear of trusting. Either way, she was grateful her stepmother had interrupted their conversation before she said any more.

"Promise?" Anna asked.

"I promise," Vivian assured her with a smile.

Vivian applied one more layer of sheer, pink gloss before putting the container in her small, pink-sequined purse. The girls admired themselves in the full-length mirror while Rebecca snapped a few candid shots.

When the doorbell rang, Anna squealed, "They're here!"

Vivian was a bit surprised to find herself practically skipping behind Anna down the hallway toward the staircase. Before Grant left that afternoon, they had both agreed that they would focus on enjoying homecoming tonight. The weight of the world, or of Heaven and Hell, as it seemed to be, would have to wait to be shouldered tomorrow.

Rebecca followed behind the girls, camera flashing.

As Vivian neared the landing, a sudden chill swept up the back of her neck. She stopped suddenly, causing Rebecca to crash into her. Vivian gazed into the pink bedroom. A dance of shadows played against the flowered wallpaper.

The room literally pulsated with the activity of dark spirits. The sounds of their labored breaths, so much like the hissing gasps her grandmother had made as her lungs were eaten away by cancer, wheezed through the air.

Rebecca followed her gaze into the room. "Do you see something?" she asked, placing a hand gently on Vivian's shoulder.

"No," Vivian lied.

She was still shaken by the morning's events. She did not understand how she could have been so wrong about Sarah's body being buried under the willow tree—but she *had* been wrong. She didn't want to bother her family with any more talk of spirits, if she couldn't rely on her ability to communicate with them to be accurate.

"Wow, Anna. You're smokin'!" Jason exclaimed with a

crooked smile.

"Not, 'you look lovely', or 'you're gorgeous'? You have to refer to me the same way you'd talk about a fried piece of bacon? So romantic," Anna quipped.

"Hey, you know how I feel about bacon. That's like the highest possible compliment."

Vivian looked down the stairs and saw Grant gazing back at her. He wore a black suit, pale gray button-up shirt, and charcoal gray tie. His smile seemed to paralyze Vivian as she returned it.

"You look beautiful." Grant's eyes sparkled in the light of the chandelier. Her father stood beside him.

"I would have to agree," he said.

"Thank you," Vivian replied. She looked back toward the pink bedroom.

Not tonight, she thought. *Tonight, I'm just a normal girl. And I'm going to the homecoming dance with the boy I have a major crush on.* She turned her gaze toward the foyer and hurried down the steps behind Anna.

The double daters hurried out the front door toward Jason's sporty, silver-blue Camaro.

"*This* is your car?" Vivian asked, the cool breeze tousling her curls slightly.

"What? You figured me as a truck boy?"

"More like a souped-up truck on some extra-tall wheels, with an American Flag painted on the tailgate. I thought Anna might have to pull out some kind of cheerleading toss to get me up to the door."

Grant pushed the front seat forward and motioned with one hand toward the back.

"After you." His dimples popped while he held Vivian's hand gently.

She steadied herself against him as she maneuvered between the seats, being careful to keep the short skirt of her dress down.

"My brother got *that* truck." Jason laughed, flashing a crooked smile. "I had to settle for the sports car."

"Thank goodness," Anna chimed in before settling into the passenger seat. "I wouldn't be caught dead going to homecoming in your brother's truck! It's ridiculous!"

"If by ridiculous you mean awesome, then I agree one hundred percent."

"Umm...yeah, that's exactly what I meant." Anna smiled over her shoulder at Vivian. "Boys and their big trucks. I'll never understand it! As long as I don't have to ride in it to the homecoming dance, I'm not going to worry about it."

"But if we go mudding some Saturday, you'll be glad we've got the truck," Jason said, shutting his door as he peered in the review mirror at Vivian. "What do you think, Vivian? Are you up for a little mud-bogging double-date action?"

"I have no idea what mud bogging is, but I suppose I'd try almost anything once."

"I'll never admit I said this, but it is actually kind of fun," Anna interjected.

Jason eyes widened as he glanced at Anna. "Last time we went, you complained the entire time about how stupid it was."

"I know, and I'll complain next time, too. But deep down, I kind of like bouncing around in that big, stupid truck while the mud flies through the air around us."

Grant nestled into the seat beside Vivian, his thigh resting gently against her leg. The warmth of his body sent heat pulsing through her like electricity. She wondered if he could hear her heart pounding against her chest. She wondered if his heart was beating just as rapidly.

Biting her lower lip gently, she smiled at him, unconsciously staring at his lips, thinking how soft they looked.

"I brought something for you." His lips moved smoothly as he wet them slightly with his tongue before parting them into a small smile.

She forced herself to look away from his mouth, afraid she might start breathing heavily if she continued to think about how nice his lips would feel pressed against her own. Gazing at his pale blue eyes, Vivian blushed, when she realized his eyes seemed to be locked on her lips as well.

He leaned over her, reaching toward the far corner of the floor. Her breath stuck in her throat as his thick chest pressed against her knees.

He sat up holding a small, brown paper bag, which rustled noisily as he reached inside. Pulling out a six pack of apple flavored juice boxes, Grant smiled proudly.

"I promised you juice boxes with dinner."

He rustled the bag again before holding up a package of Ho Hos.

"And for dessert."

Vivian's smile threatened to split her cheeks as she laughed.

Jason glanced into the review mirror as he shifted the Camaro into drive.

"You brought a sack lunch for dinner?" Smiling broadly at Anna he said, "Would you settle for a happy meal from the drive-thru? No one told me it was a brown-bag dinner date."

"Don't even think about it. You owe me a nice dinner from Luciano's. It's part of the homecoming date deal. And I get to order anything I want, including dessert," she winked as she patted his leg.

The Camaro moved forward down the lane, while Grant slipped the Ho Hos and juice boxes back into the bag before setting it in the corner of the seat beside him. He moved closer to Vivian, their legs still touching lightly, and reached for her hand. She felt his damp palm against her own as his fingers laced with hers. As she snuggled her shoulder against his chest, the willows speeding past the windows, she could feel his heart thumping beneath his shirt.

"Thanks for agreeing to come with me to the dance," he whispered, his minty breath tickling the side of Vivian's cheek.

"Thanks for asking me," she replied, turning her head to look into his eyes. "Going to homecoming tonight almost makes me feel normal again."

"Well, promise not to get too normal."

"I think we both know, that's not even remotely possible." Vivian laughed.

Grant squeezed her hand tightly before leaning in and letting his lips press gently against hers. She thought her heart might explode as it somehow managed to beat even faster than it had been before. He pulled back and softly kissed her forehead.

Tonight, she would pretend to be normal. She would not let herself wonder about the shadows hovering around her peers. She would pay absolutely no attention to the guardian spirits who lingered beside the girls in pretty dresses and the boys with color-coordinated ties. She would simply be a girl on a date with a boy. drinking juice boxes and eating Ho Hos in a small town's lone fine Italian restaurant.

It couldn't be too hard to play normal for one night. And even though Grant knew a smidgen of the truth, he seemed content to play along with her, at least for the evening. She knew tomorrow she'd have to face the demons that haunted her, but she also knew she didn't have to face them alone.

She kissed Grant's cheek gently before snuggling back into the crook of his neck.

VIVIAN HAD LOOKED EXQUISITE as she bounded down the front steps of her house. The makeup she wore made her eyes look even bigger than usual. The curls of her hair framed her high cheekbones and those incredibly big, doe eyes.

They found themselves holding their breath as they

watched her.

She had put so much effort into looking just right.

What a perfect way to die, they thought.

So pretty. So full of life—for now. They had hunted long enough. Tonight was the night they had been waiting for so patiently. Finally, all their planning would come together.

CHAPTER TWENTY-TWO

WITH THE FLUORESCENT LIGHTS OFF AND the disco balls flashing, the commons felt like a night club, or what Vivian assumed a night club would feel like. She had never been to one herself, but some of her friends back home would go on teen night. Unfortunately, Vivian's mother had always said no. She said she would reconsider when Vivian turned seventeen.

Her seventeenth birthday was just a few months away. Her mother wouldn't be there to make her a cake or wish her a happy birthday. She would never get to reconsider letting her go to the night club.

There was no point in asking her father to reconsider in her mother's place. Richfield only had one dumpy bar. Vivian was pretty sure it didn't boast a disco ball, and they had probably never even heard of teen night.

Grant high-fived a few fellow football players as they made their way toward the far corner of the transformed commons, where a handful of teachers manned a table of punch and cookies. The open space which served as Richfield High School's dining hall during the lunch hours and a study hall at various periods in the afternoon, now sparkled with twinkling trees posted along the wall. The exposed brick had been draped with pale blue fabric.

"Can I get you some?" Grant asked, motioning toward the food and beverage tables.

"Sure. That would be great."

He shook his head slightly as he gazed at her for a few extra seconds.

"What?" she asked self-consciously.

"You are just so beautiful. I mean, seriously, insanely beautiful."

Her cheeks flushed as she twisted at her curls. "Well, I took a shower for tonight. And it's not every day I curl my hair and layer on the makeup."

"You don't need all that. I mean, the shower's a good idea, but the rest of it—totally unnecessary. I shake my head at how gorgeous you are when your hair's pulled back in gym class and you've got sweat dripping off your nose."

"Hey, that only happens when Mr. Jackson makes us run around the gym ten times. And I do not sweat. I get dewy. It's totally different."

Grant laughed. "Whatever you call it, it's hot."

He paused, gazing at her. His look turned from flirty to worried.

"You can leave me for two minutes to grab us refreshments. The boogeyman won't hurt me in this crowd," she said, trying to make light of his worried expression.

He didn't move.

"Go. It's been an hour since my snack cake and juice box. I'm in serious danger of a sugar crash."

"Okay, but don't move," he said, slowly backing away. "I'll be right back."

She wasn't a fan of anyone treating her like she wasn't capable of taking care of herself, but as she watched him glance over his shoulder more times than she could count while making his way through the tangle of bodies dressed in sparkles and crisply-pressed cotton, she couldn't help but smile.

When he returned, Grant was balancing two cups of punch on top of a cookie in each hand. Another cookie protruded from his mouth. It wobbled on his lips as he grinned playfully at Vivian. Pulling it from his mouth, she took a bite.

"Yum." She winked at him as she chewed.

Jason grabbed a cookie from Grant's hand. "If a girl likes your slobbery cookie, I think there's a good chance she'd like a big ol' slobbery kiss from you, too."

Vivian blushed. Grant shook his head, rolling his eyes in amusement.

"Bashly, you're kind of the opposite of smooth."

"Is this smooth?" Jason wrapped his arms around Anna, who feigned protest as she giggled. "Want some of my cookie, baby?"

"I think I'll pass." She laughed, as he opened his mouth in front of her, a half-chewed cookie stuck to his teeth.

"Maybe later." He winked as he took her hand and moved toward the crowded dance floor. "I think it's time to get shakin', bacon."

"You're still referring to me as a slab of pig fat?" She rolled her eyes as she followed him into the crowd.

Several girls stood in a cluster near the football players Grant had greeted when they'd first stepped into the dance. Vivian assumed they were their dates. She recognized a couple as members of the cheerleading squad. The group whispered as they gave Vivian sideways glances.

Vivian shifted uncomfortably under the weight of their stares as the music pulsed through her body. She sipped on her punch and pretended not to notice them.

When the music's rhythm slowed, Grant took the half empty cup from Vivian's hand and set it on a nearby table. He winked as he pulled her toward the dance floor.

"Coming through," he said, as the crowd of gawking girls parted for them to pass. He put his hand on the small of her back, pulling her body close to his. Her skin felt electric when his cheek brushed against hers. Her breath caught in her throat as his breath tickled her ear.

As she wrapped her arms around his neck, he looked into her eyes and pressed his forehead against hers. Their bodies swayed to the rhythm. The slow song didn't last long enough, and too soon the beat quickened. The bodies around them began to bounce with the new cadence. But Vivian and Grant remain locked in the slow dance until Jason bounded out of the crowd of thumping bodies.

"Flying burrito!" Jason yelled as he body slammed into Grant, sending Vivian jolting out of his arms.

Grant shook his head, watching Jason bounce around him with the music.

"Where's Anna?" Vivian asked Jason as his body kept time with the music, up and down, his hair flapping with each jump.

"She had to take a whiz."

"Girl's don't whiz, we tinkle."

"Alright, she's in the can tinkling."

"Well, I'm going to the little girls' room to powder my nose."

"Code for: she's going to take a whiz," Jason said. Vivian rolled her eyes and flashed a playful grin at Grant. He grabbed her hand, his brow furrowed.

"I sort of have to use the restroom without a body guard." She squeezed his hand gently before letting go and shimmying through the crowd of dancing students.

Just as she emerged from the mass of pulsating bodies, someone tapped her shoulder. Hailey stood behind her, biting her quivering lip.

Not this again, Vivian thought.

She forced a smile, and said, "Hi, Hailey."

"Hey," she replied quietly. "I'm really…" Her lips moved but the bass of the latest dance song swallowed her words. She squeezed her eyes shut for a moment and mouthed, "Can I talk to you?"

Vivian looked toward the bathroom, hoping Anna might come out and save her from the awkwardness of the moment. A pack of girls squeezed through the door in unison as they giggled.

No Anna.

"Sure," Vivian reluctantly replied.

Hailey walked toward the double doors leading to the gymnasium wing of the school and pushed one open. Vivian had never seen them shut before.

Vivian hesitated in the threshold of the doorway. Something made her want to back away from the darkness of the hallway leading toward the girls' locker room. Maybe it was simply because Vivian assumed the doors had been shut to discourage people from leaving the commons area, and she felt badly about being there, when she probably shouldn't be.

But Hailey wanted to tell her something, and for some reason, Vivian couldn't help but feel sorry for her. So she followed her into the empty corridor.

The blare of music became a muffled series of thumps as the door clicked shut behind her. The hallway was dark, except for the light leaking through the windows of the metal doors they had just entered. The lights flashed and twirled, sending a cascade of shadows dancing along the walls of the hallway.

"Look, Vivian, I'm really sorry about yesterday in the locker room. We shouldn't have ganged up on you. I'm just…" Her words trailed off as she fought to hold back tears. "I'm just having a hard time accepting that Grant and I broke up."

"I know, Hailey. I'm sorry it's been so hard on you."

Vivian did feel badly for Hailey. She'd had a boyfriend for nine months last year. When he broke up with her, she was heartbroken. When he started dating her friend, she was pretty sure the world was going to end. Now she was on the other side of the situation. She could empathize with Hailey and didn't want to hurt her. But she liked Grant too much not to see where their relationship might go.

"Seeing you guys together tonight...he looks happy. I haven't seen him look that happy in a long time." Hailey looked down at her feet as she mumbled, "Anyway, I just wanted to tell you that I'm sorry."

"I really do understand, Hailey. Apology accepted."

"Thanks," Hailey replied with a hint of a grin. "I better get back to the dance."

As Vivian nodded in response, her phone vibrated in her small purse. She pulled it out and looked at the screen. It was a text message from Anna.

When she looked up, Hailey was gone. The double door leading to the dance, clicked shut behind her.

Vivian read the text. *Where are you?*

She texted back. *Got sidetracked by Hailey on the way to the bathroom. Be right there.*

As she slid the phone back into her purse, she saw movement at the end of the hallway out of the corner of her eye. She squinted, peering into the darkness toward the locker rooms. The outline of a body was barely visible in the near blackness.

"Vivian," a voice whispered. The sound echoed off the brick walls. It was so quiet the words were almost inaudible.

"Who's there?" Vivian strained to see the figure more clearly.

"Help me, Vivian," the voice whispered quietly again.

"Nancy, is that you?" Vivian took a few steps toward the voice.

"Hurry, Vivian. I need your help!" The whisper was quiet, but urgent.

Vivian took a few more hesitant steps toward the figure.

Shadow creatures slid across the floor and wrapped themselves around Vivian's legs, as the figure who had been whispering to her was suddenly upon her, something in their hands pulled tightly around Vivian's neck.

The hallway began to spin around her, a blur of shadows and a face she could not quite see. The blur became blackness, as Vivian gasped for air and her body became limp.

She saw only darkness. She heard a gravely laugh and felt hot, moist breath against her face.

"Gotcha," the voice hissed.

Vivian's mind turned to black as her body dropped, motionless into the arms of the unknown creature who had stalked her silently in the shadows since the moment she first stepped out of her father's car. Now the predator held its prey, helpless and vulnerable in its arms.

"YOU MADE THAT TOO easy, Vivian." They laughed as they drug her listless body through the loading dock doors. "You should never trust anything you can't see."

They threw her body over their shoulder like a rag doll as they carried her down a few steps. A cool breeze stirred a pile of leaves that had nestled against the base of the stairs.

Using one finger, they pressed a button on a set of keys clasped in the palm of their hand and popped the trunk of a car waiting at the end of the dock. Vivian's body met the inside of the trunk with a thud. She moaned as the lid slammed shut above her.

CHAPTER TWENTY-THREE

VIVIAN RUBBED HER NECK AS HER eyes fluttered open.

What happened?

She lay on her stomach, her cheek pressed against the cool ground. The unmistakable smell of moist dirt filled her nostrils.

Where am I?

As she pushed her body up, her head pulsed with pain. The hem of her dress tore under the weight of her body as she strained to pull herself off the ground. She slipped on the torn fabric, fumbling to rise to an upright position.

She sensed their presence, before she saw them—heard their breathing. A quiet wheeze of air. In, then out. The hairs rose along the back of her throbbing neck. Her hand rubbed at the tender flesh which had been bruised and scratched, as she was choked into unconsciousness.

Her surroundings were nearly void of any light. Thin streaks of illumination bled through the planks of wood above her, allowing Vivian to see the knotty beam supports of a ceiling.

A cellar. She must be in a cellar somewhere.

As her eyes adjusted to the lack of light, she saw a shadow creature slithering toward her like an onyx snake. Instinctively, she pulled away from the form that writhed inches from her face. As it hissed, the smell of decay emanated from the black hole of its mouth. A serpent tongue licked at Vivian's face before the beast disappeared back into the darkness of the room.

"Ah, you're finally awake," a thin voice murmured from somewhere deep within the shadows. Vivian spun her head around too quickly, searching the darkness. For several seconds, she held her head in her hands as she tried to stop the blackness around her from spinning.

The boards above her crawled with shadows. They dangled from beams as they reached toward her, causing the dank air around her to whirl with an unearthly chill that made her flesh ache.

"I was afraid you'd never wake up. That would be a shame. I'm not ready to be done with you, yet." The voice was as light as a sprinkle of rain on a window pane. Though Vivian strained to hear the words, they seemed to bounce off the walls around her, making it impossible for her to tell where the voice was coming from.

Vivian could not place the voice as being male or female. There was a growl rattling under the whispered words that made her wonder for a moment if it was even human.

Her heart pounding in her chest, Vivian wiped at hot tears with trembling hands, as she strained to see into the deep darkness of the damp, musty cellar. Very slowly, she inched back on her hands and knees like a frightened animal backing away from a hungry wolf, bumping into a row of shelves. Jars rattled above her.

A low laugh rippled through the stale air. It was the menacing laugh of pure insanity.

"Who...who...are you?" Vivian stammered as she slowly rose to her feet. "Where...am I?"

"I am the one who watches you," the whisper scratched at the air ominously with a hint of melody. "And you are right where I want you."

Footsteps scuffed across the dirt floor.

For a few terrifying moments, Vivian was certain whoever was holding her hostage was getting closer. Her eyes widened as she held her breath and watched the darkness for someone to reach out at her.

Wood creaked as her unseen tormentor ascended a set of steps. A door in the ceiling lifted. Dull moonlight illuminated the stairwell. Someone stood in the light for a moment. The outline of a human form, which was cloaked by the darkness of several shadow figures, hovered for a moment before disappearing through the hole.

The door slammed shut, leaving Vivian concealed in the darkness of the cellar.

She let her breath quiver past her lips as a mild sense of relief washed over her. She was alone, and for the moment she was safe.

Metal screeched against metal as a bolt was slid into place. She had been in this room before—not for very long, but she recognized the steps leading to the trap door. She was in the room beneath the coal shed.

Vivian stumbled around the cellar, her hands groping at the air until she reached the shelves. Her fingers slid across the smooth, cold glass of jars. She hadn't noticed the shelves of jars the last time she had been in the space. Her eyes tried to adjust to the coal blackness of the room. Her breath came in ragged gasps as she felt for something—anything she could use to defend herself when her attacker returned.

"I have to find a way out." Vivian slowed her breath, trying to calm herself enough to think straight.

"The only way out is through that door in the ceiling." Thane's voice broke the silence.

"The door to the tunnel…"

"It's blocked. Raymond bricked both doors to the tunnel."

"Are you sure?" Vivian felt her heart race as panic set in. "There has to be another way. A window maybe."

"There's nothing, Vivian." For the first time ever, Thane's voice frightened her. Fear wrapped around his words, making them shrill and tight with tension. He was just as afraid as she was.

"What can I do, Thane?"

"Pray, Vivian. There's nothing else you can do right now."

Vivian dropped to the ground, her bare knees pressed into the cool, damp earth beneath her. For the first time since her mother and her brother had been killed, she cried out to God for help.

The words tumbled past her lips in rapid, desperate whispers as she pleaded.

"Please don't let me die!" she begged.

Vivian felt swallowed by the darkness as she huddled on the floor. Her eyes burned from crying. Taking several deep breathes she fought to control her terror.

"I have to think. I'm not giving up. There has to be some way out of here." The words quivered quietly past her lips as she peered into the deep dark of the room.

With the slivers of light creeping through the floor boards, Vivian was able to find a wall. Stumbling across the uneven dirt, she walked the perimeter of the cellar, feeling for a window or a door. There was nothing. Just the bricked up doorway and rows and rows of shelves filled with jars. She imagined the jars to be filled with macabre animal fetuses or disembodied limbs of long dead creatures.

The creaks and moans of the floor above had ceased. Silence hung in the air like a thick, menacing cloud, threatening to burst open with a torrential downpour of horror.

With each wall inspected, she began to crawl from one side of the room to the other, using the thin lines of light above as a guide to help her make straight rows back and forth across the cellar floor. Her hands, caked in dirt, groped in the dimness for anything she might be able to use to protect herself.

She wondered if anyone was looking for her. Maybe Grant had called her father as soon as he'd realized she wasn't coming back from the bathroom. Maybe there was a search party combing through the town, searching for any sign of where she could have gone.

Time no longer had meaning to Vivian. She could have been locked in the cellar for an hour. Maybe it had been several hours. She had no way of knowing how long she had been unconscious. By the time she had crossed most of the room, her knees scraped and bleeding from crawling across rocks that protruded from the dirt beneath her, she imagined it was late into the night. Maybe it was even morning.

She paused to listen for any sign of birds chirping beyond the confines of the chilled brick walls. The silence was eerie. The kind of dead calm that almost never happens naturally. No crickets, or birds, or creatures of any kind made noises in or around the cellar.

Vivian understood animals had ways of sensing the spirits moving around humans. She wondered if the dark spirits clinging to her captor had frightened even the crickets away.

She had noticed the same strange quiet around her father's home. Where there should have been the quaver of frogs calling into the night, there was silence. Dead, unnatural silence.

She rose onto her knees then dropped heavily back to the ground. She again pleaded with God to help her, and another wave of warm tears rolled down her cheeks as the grimness of her situation sank in.

"God, if I'm going to die, please let it be fast." Her throat tightened as she spoke the words out loud. The realization she might soon be with her mother, away from the heartache that had consumed her soul for so many months, comforted her a little.

"Vivian, you can't give up. It's not your time, yet. You have to fight," said Thane.

"I don't want to give up, but I don't know what to do. There's no way out." She bit her trembling lip. "I can't find a stick or a rock or anything big enough to defend myself with."

"I found a light in the middle of the room. I'll help you find it. There has to be something down here that can help us. Go straight from where you're sitting."

The moist dirt stung her torn flesh as she crawled across the floor.

"How much farther?"

"Not much. Stop. It's right above you."

Slowly, Vivian stood and raised her hands above her head, sweeping them through the air in search of a cord she could pull that would switch on the light. She felt a string brush the back of her hand. Her other hand grasped at the air, knocking into the cord, causing it to swing back and forth. Wildly, her hands swatted at the air, occasionally brushing the cord with her skin as it swung past. When it finally hit her palm, she gripped her fingers tightly around it and pulled.

Yellow light shattered the darkness. The sudden jolt of brightness sent Vivian stumbling backward. She squeezed her eyes shut for a moment, before snapping them open, wide and filled with terror, as she scanned her surroundings.

The hazy glow filled the small space with shadows—still, unmoving shadows cast by rickety wooden shelves filled with jars of tomatoes and green beans. Pieces of a broken rocking chair were stacked under the wooden, planked steps leading to the door in the ceiling. Exposed bricks lined the walls, red clay crumbling off in several spots.

Vivian stumbled toward the blocked passage and pressed on the fresh, red bricks. They were solid, nothing like the bricks she had torn her way through before. Those bricks had come down so easily, almost as if an unseen force helped her rip the wall down. But there was no force helping her now. She pressed her head against the fresh mortar and cried.

In the corner farthest from the steps, something glinted in the light. Vivian strained to see what it was. Something silver, lying on top of a small rise in the dirt floor. The ground beneath the object appeared disturbed. It was mounded slightly higher than the soil around it.

"What is that?" Thane stood beside her, looking toward the mound of dirt.

Vivian reluctantly moved across the room. The heels of her black, glittery shoes sunk into the ground as if they were trying to hold her back. When her toes touched the edge of the mound, she dropped to her knees.

With a trembling hand, she picked up the object glimmering on top of the heaped soil. It clattered as she grasped it in her hand. Her mouth dropped open, but nothing more than a long, shaky breath emerged. Her entire body quaked with horror as she stared at the disturbed earth in front of her.

"It's Sarah's bracelet."

"The one Anna picked up last night under the willow tree?"

"Yes." She gagged as she choked back the bile rising into her throat. "And...she's here."

"Can she help us?"

"Not her spirit," Vivian replied. "Her body."

Thane peered down. A small piece of pale, blue fabric and a dust covered bone peeked above the mound. Vivian cupped her hands over her mouth as her body heaved. Turning her face away from the grisly sight, she vomited.

Once again, Vivian faced the harsh reality of death. The pretty young girl, who's spirit she had come to know, was now nothing more than dirty bones, still clothed in the pajamas she had put on one evening to wear to sleep—never knowing they would become her burial gown.

Vivian vomited until she collapsed in an exhausted heap beside Sarah's grave. She wept for Sarah and for herself, fearing that her body, shrouded in a sparkly homecoming dress, might soon rest beside Sarah's. Rotting away—the flesh picked at by larvae and creatures that lived in cold, dark places. Until she too became nothing more than dirty bones.

CHAPTER TWENTY-FOUR

LYING AT THE BASE OF SARAH'S crude grave, Vivian's heart raced as she moved the heart pendent between her fingers.

"Why did she show me she was buried under the willow tree by the pond?" Vivian wondered aloud.

"Maybe she was," Thane speculated. *"If someone moved my body from my grave right now, I'm not sure I would know where they moved me to because my spirit isn't with my body. I was there when they buried me, but now I'm with you."*

"Maybe that's why the shadows have such a strong hold on Sarah. She's confused because she doesn't know where her body is. Someone must have moved her at some point, and when she couldn't find herself, the confusion and fear made her spirit weak."

Several moments later, the silence was broken by the squeaking hinges on a door. Dust dropped from the wooden beams of the ceiling as heavy footsteps crossed the room above her. The sound of something banging against the wall was followed by a hollow thud against the wooden floor.

"Crap," a voice mumbled. Their body scuffed against the dust-covered planks as they seemed to be picking themselves up from falling down.

Then silence.

Vivian listened to the silence. She wanted to shout, hoping that it was someone who was looking for her, but the fear that it might be her captor sealed her throat shut, trapping her screams for help. The voice was too muffled to recognize, but she was certain it was a male.

It was probably only seconds that passed as she waited, but time seemed to stop. Holding her breath, she strained to hear any noise from above her. She heard footsteps hesitantly cross the small room, before the cracks in the boards above her became veined with light.

The deadbolt in the trap door screeched as it was unlatched. Vivian's heart throbbed inside her chest, which felt tight and ached as if her skin was suddenly too small for her body. She squinted against the sudden brightness of the room above her where the light had been switched on. Her eyes widened in fear as she saw the shiny, black shoes of a man step into the shadows of the staircase.

"Vivian?" Grant's voice called into the cellar. "Are you in here?"

He stepped in further and swept the ray of a large, silver flashlight he held in his hand across the dirt floored room.

"Grant?" Vivian's voice came out like a whimper. Tears began to flow down her muddied cheeks again as she crawled across the dirt floor, still unsure she could trust her own hearing to be certain it was Grant who had just called her name into the tomb she had been trapped in.

Grant hurried down the steps, his flashlight pointed at her as he rushed toward her. She squeezed her eyes shut against the bright light. In that single second, with her senses shut back into the darkness created by her eyelids, she heard a sickening crack, followed by the thud of a body hitting the floor.

Vivian opened her eyes to see Grant sprawled out on the

cold, hard ground, a small pool of blood already forming around the top of his head. The flashlight he had been carrying spun in a circle on the floor a few feet away from him, making the room dance in the dull yellow light.

Jason stood above Grant, looking down at him. For a moment she thought of running to Jason, screaming for him to get out, because the person who had just knocked Grant to the floor, the same person who had kidnapped her and locked her in Sarah Christian's grave, might hurt him, too. But the hollow look in Jason's eyes as he shifted his gaze from Grant to Vivian made her step back deeper into the gloom of the cellar. And then she noticed the silver blade of the shovel he held in his hand glinting in the quavering light of Grant's flashlight.

As Vivian took a few hesitant steps away from Jason, shadows emerged from every corner of the cellar and slithered around Jason's legs. She could hear them purr as they slid up his back, covering Jason's shoulders like a black cloak.

Jason's eyes fixed on Vivian as his expression became void of any emotion. His pupils had become like black holes, as the dark spirits whispered muffled words into his ear. The shovel dropped to the ground beside Grant's body.

A menacing grin twisted Jason's face. His lips parted in a thin smile just before a low giggle slipped past them. The sound made Vivian's skin crawl with fear.

"Poor Grant."

A deep whisper filled the room. It was the same inhuman voice she had heard hours earlier, when she had awoken on the floor of the cellar.

"He always wants to save them, but he never can."

"What have you done, Jason? Grant's your friend." Her voice squeaked from her mouth, little more than a whimper.

"Of course, he is, Vivian," Jason replied, a spark of emotion glinting in his eyes. "I would never want to hurt *him*." Jason shook his head as he looked down at Grant's unmoving body. "It's *you* I want."

Jason stepped over Grant's body then stopped, looking back at him sadly.

"Why do you always have to try to be the hero," he mumbled, before returning his menacing stare to Vivian.

Raising an eyebrow, Jason regarded Vivian sadly. "Now I have to kill both of you."

Jason looked solemnly at the crude grave behind Vivian.

"I see you found Sarah. I had to move her from under the willow tree. After the snow melted, Anna kept going out there. For a while, I thought she knew."

He took a step toward Vivian.

"And then your dad moved in. Anna told me he'd asked Raymond to block up the passageway, and he wanted this old shed knocked down."

Jason glanced back at Sarah's decayed remains and shook his head as he eyed the vomit near them. "It's not very polite to throw up on someone's final resting place.

He took a step toward Vivian. "But I suppose I can't blame you. Sarah was a bit disgusting. The way she and Grant were messing around with each other behind Hailey's back, and then she pretended to be Hailey's friend."

The shadows slithered around his body like a bed of black snakes.

"And Nancy—she just had to get her claws into Grant as soon as she heard he was single. The day after Grant and Hailey broke up, Nancy waited for him after football practice, giving him some sob story about not having a ride home. Of course, Grant gave her a ride..."

Jason bit his lip until blood dripped from the corner of his mouth.

"They always wanted Grant. And he already had someone."

Vivian glanced at the broken chair wedged under the steps behind Jason. She inched slowly to her right, hoping she might be able to move around him and get to it. Maybe she could use a piece of the wood to defend herself against the monster the boy she'd come to know and like had become.

"They wanted him instead of you." Vivian's voice quivered, terror tugging at her vocal chords with each word.

"You know, it's not fair for one person to be so good at *everything*—Richfield's golden boy. Girls just throw themselves at him. And he had Hailey, his female counter-part."

Rage creased his forehead. His jaw tensed. "If I had a girl like Hailey, I wouldn't let any of those whores get in the way."

Jason's eyes were wild with anger, as he scratched at his forearms. Blood began to seep through the crisp, white shirt he'd worn for the homecoming dance.

"I'm sure lots of girls like you, Jason. You're every bit as good as Grant."

"You could have liked me, but you went straight for Grant," Jason said, glaring at Vivian. "You're just like the rest of them." Jason pressed his palms into his temples, his body shaking with anger.

"I do like you, Jason." Vivian sidestepped slowly away from the wall, trying to inch around him. "I just...didn't think you'd be interested in me."

Jason's glare cut through the haziness of the cellar. "I'm not stupid, Vivian."

He moved forward, closing the gap between the two of them. "Why are all the whores so pretty?"

The demon on his shoulder hissed and extended its clawed fingers toward Vivian's face. She shuddered as the coldness of its touch caressed her check. Jason's hand reached toward Vivian, becoming one with the shadow.

He placed his other hand on Vivian's cheek. Gently, he held her face in his hands. Looking into Vivian's eyes, a sick smile warped his features as he rasped, "I wonder how pretty you'll look when you're dead."

Before Vivian could react, Jason's hands slid around her neck and squeezed.

Grabbing Jason's wrists, Vivian tried to pull his hands away. But the spirits fueled Jason with a superhuman strength that Vivian could not match. Her lungs tightened as she gasped for air. The lack of oxygen dropped her to her knees. Jason's face twisted and blurred as he stared down into Vivian's eyes.

Vivian pleaded for Jason to stop with soundless words. Her lips tinged blue as she mouthed, "No. Please..."

Something struck Jason on the shoulder, causing him to loosen his death grip. Vivian slumped forward. Her face met the dirt floor with a dull thud.

For a moment, her spirit slipped away from her body. She floated above herself and saw her motionless shape heaped on the floor just a few feet away from Grant's unmoving body. Frantically, she looked around the cellar. Shadows filled the space, crawling across the floor, scaling the walls, hanging from the rafters in the ceiling. Dozens of dark spirits—writhing and seething at Vivian's lifeless form.

The sound of shattering glass pulled Vivian back to her body as she sucked the stale air of the cellar into her lungs. Her chest ached as she coughed. The ground around her had become wet. Green beans and chunks of tomatoes rolled through puddles of mud.

With bleary eyes, Vivian looked up to see Jason shielding himself from the jars being hurled at him.

"Who's doing that?" he shrieked. "Stop it!"

A gentle hand touched Vivian's shoulder. With supernatural strength, Thane lifted her to her feet. His body felt as solid as her own, as he held her up. The dark spirits wailed in protest when he helped her walk toward the steps.

While he led her up the stairs, nearly carrying her entire weight, she peered back into the chaos of the cellar. Jars flew off the shelves as the spirits of Nancy and Sarah heaved them with hands that Jason could not see.

The dark masses of bestial creatures swirled and hissed

through the room, a torrent of evil spinning hate and anger like a cyclone.

"She's getting away!" the demonic voices howled in unison—a choir of terror screaming through the madness of Jason's shrieks and shattering glass.

Jason spun on his heels, his eyes wild as he glared at Vivian. He rushed to the steps, jars crashing behind him. Blood began to rise through his white shirt where shards of glass had sliced through his skin. Vivian's body, still numb from oxygen deprivation, stumbled up the steps while Thane trembled under her weight, helping her along.

"I'm losing my strength," he said, his voice like a trickle of water.

Jason threw himself at Vivian, clamping onto her ankles, his fingernails clawing into her flesh. Simultaneous howls of anger and panic pulsated through the small room as they slid down the wooden steps. Their bodies crashed against the dried, cracked wood.

Vivian's nails splintered as she clawed at the steps, desperate to stop her rapid descent. Jason seemed to climb Vivian as he pulled her thrashing body back into the cellar. Pressing his weight against Vivian's body, he grabbed a fistful of her hair and thrust her forehead against the front edge of a step. Blood trickled over Vivian's brow as she moaned and clawed at Jason's fingers, which were wound tightly within her hair.

Disoriented, Vivian was flung backwards off the last few steps and landed with a dull thud onto her back. Jason moved quickly over her, a shard of glass clenched in his right hand. Blood streamed down his arm, the sleeve of his shirt had become more red than white, as the glass cut into his own flesh.

Jason dropped to his knees, pinning Vivian beneath him. Hand raised above his head, his hollow eyes stared unblinking into Vivian's. A drop of blood splashed onto Vivian's forehead as she looked up at the glass dagger.

"Please, Jason. Don't..." her trembling voice pleaded. It could have belonged to a stranger—Vivian didn't recognize the high-pitched sound begging for her life. "Please."

Jason caressed Vivian's cheek with his left hand as he used his other hand to press the edge of the broken glass against her neck. "Still so pretty."

Vivian felt the glass stab into her throat. Hot blood trickled around the back of her neck. She heard her own screams, like an animal helplessly caught in a trap—no words, just wild howls of terror. She did not close her eyes. She stared into the cold, empty face of a killer, who looked back at her as if possessed by the Devil himself.

Jason's body lurched forward as a loud thwack penetrated through Vivian's screams. Something had struck him in the head. The sudden blow sent him tumbling off of Vivian. The shard of glass fell into Vivian's hair, which partially covered her face—a mess of tangles caked with dirt and soaked in blood.

Her father's face appeared above her. His eyes could not hide the horror he felt as he looked at her blood covered face and neck. Dropping the shovel he was holding, he tore the sleeve from his shirt and pressed the fabric against Vivian's neck.

"You're going to be alright."

"Dad..." Her eyes felt heavy as she struggled to keep them open.

"Stay with me, Vivian!"

Her eyes fluttered open. She tried to speak, but was too weak to push the words across her lips.

"I'm here. I won't let you go."

Across the room, Raymond struggled to hold Jason against the floor. His howls ripped through the cellar—the screams of a dozen demons cried out through the voice of a boy gone mad. The black spirits that had clung to Jason swirled above him—a dark cloud of screeches and gnashing teeth.

Thane's spirit knelt beside Vivian. Putting his hand on top of his father's, he pressed the blood soaked cloth into Vivian's neck.

James looked up, and Vivian realized from the expression on her father's face that he could see Thane. For a moment her father was face to face with his dead son. She saw Thane's blue eyes light up, and he raised one side of his mouth into a lopsided smile, as he seemed to understand that his father could see him.

"It's not her time. She'll be okay," Thane murmured to their father, soft and reassuring. *"I love you, Dad."*

Vivian watched the look of pure joy and wonder cross her father's face. "I love you, too, Thane," he murmured back, his voice catching on the words.

"Thane," Vivian moaned dully. She could hear sirens getting closer. She closed her eyes.

"Stay with me, Vivian. Don't leave me."

Darkness swallowed Vivian as her father's voice faded into the blackness of her mind. There was no sound. No light or color. Only darkness so thick it was beyond black. It was nothing.

CHAPTER TWENTY-FIVE

SNOW CRUNCHED BENEATH VIVIAN'S FEET AS she wound through the bare trees behind her father's house. A light dusting of white clung to the green needles of the pine trees as she maneuvered past them. When she reached the clearing in front of the small, ice-covered pond, she paused.

Stooping at the base of the willow tree, she placed a pair of bright-pink Gerbera daisies on the blanket of snow covering the spot where, only a few months before, her father had stood in a gaping hole as he dug in search of Sarah's body. The dirt had since been replaced and would be reseeded after the spring thaw.

Although Sarah's remains had been moved to a cemetery shortly after the police finished their investigation, and her spirit no longer lingered in or around the home, Vivian wanted to honor the spot which had served as her original grave. Rebecca had offered to help her plant a small patch of perennials near the base of the willow tree after the snow melted, and they'd placed a small bench beneath the shade of the low hanging branches, where both Anna and Vivian often sat to read on warm days—sometimes together, sometimes alone.

Before the winter chill had set in, her father had placed a brass bell secured to a four foot high stake in the ground near the willow tree. After Grandma May passed away, Vivian's mother had put a similar bell in her flower garden.

"Whenever we think of her, we can ring this bell. She'll hear it all the way up in Heaven, and she'll know we haven't forgotten her," her mother had explained.

Vivian gently tugged the thin, braided chord that made the bell sing. The sound sent a woodpecker scuttling from his home in the trunk of a nearby oak tree. Vivian had come to expect the beat of his black and white wings flapping past her each Friday.

This had become her routine. Two pink flowers to honor the girls she had never known in life, but whose spirits had reached out to her beyond death. A few moments to quietly think about her mother and brother. And a quick jingle of the bell to send her thoughts of love to them all in Heaven.

As the sound of the ringing bell climbed higher and was swallowed by the dusky sky, Vivian began the short walk back toward the house. Midway along the path, she glanced at her watch, and then began to jog the rest of the way as the purple-orange sunlight slipped behind the barn in the horizon.

Rushing through the back door, she slipped off the rubber boots and set them on the doormat, then hung the oversized, down-filled coat on the hook in the wall. She found Rebecca and her father drinking tea at the kitchen table.

Rebecca's eyes brightened as Vivian sat down beside her. She reached for the hairbrush sitting on the table beside a small container of bobby pins and hair bands.

"Ready?" she asked as she rose to her feet and stood behind Vivian.

"Work your magic."

Vivian grimaced as Rebecca worked the brush through her hair. After several minutes of tugging, Rebecca snapped the clear elastic band around the end of the loose braid she had twisted into Vivian's light brown tresses.

"James, look at your daughter! Isn't she beautiful?"

Rebecca held a small mirror in front of Vivian.

"Nice work, Rebecca! I love it." She moved the braid slightly closer to her face, covering the half-inch, shiny, pink scar on the side of her neck—a grim reminder of the attack she had suffered a few months before. Her left hand moved a few pieces of hair strategically in front of the thickened white line that ran above her eye—another bad memory.

Looking up from the newspaper, James smiled.

"Wow!" he exclaimed, cocking an eyebrow. "Is that mascara on your eyelashes? You hardly ever wear makeup."

"Dad, I'm going on a date. I think that qualifies as a good time to slop a little paint on the barn."

Thane appeared behind her, looking over her shoulder into the mirror. *"Trying to hide your battle scars?"*

"These scars make me look like a road map," Vivian mumbled under her breath in response to her brother's words that only she could hear.

"You shouldn't try to hide them. I think they make you look bad ass."

"Just a couple reminders that God has something special planned for you, so He has to keep you around here," her father said from behind his paper, oblivious to Thane's presence.

"Yeah, I suppose that's a nicer way to put it. But they also say, don't mess with me 'cause I will beat you down!"

Vivian let out a small giggle.

The doorbell rang, sending Vivian to her feet. James looked at Rebecca, raising a brow.

"Did I say something funny? I was trying to be serious."

"She's a teenager. I don't think we're capable of fully understanding." She placed one hand to the side of her mouth dramatically, as if trying to hide her words and whispered,

"We're old."

"Well, help me to my feet, Grandma. Let's go see these whippersnappers off."

They walked toward the entryway, James's arm draped over Rebecca's shoulder—her arm wrapped around his waist. Vivian threw open the front door, revealing Grant with a bouquet of flowers in one hand.

"Ah, James, he brought her flowers!" Rebecca gushed.

"Actually, Mrs. Bennett, these are for you." Grant extended the bouquet toward her.

"Well, that's very nice, Grant," James replied. He patted Grant's shoulder and smiled. "Vivian's curfew is still midnight."

"I'll have her home by eleven-forty-five. Promise."

Vivian shook her head as she slipped on a pair of mittens and hurried across the foyer.

"Have fun," Rebecca said flashing a smile.

Vivian skipped down the steps of the front porch. The cool, winter breeze tickled her face with the loose hairs that whipped around her cheeks. Grant opened the passenger door, and she slipped into the seat, grateful to be out of the cold. As he walked around the back of the car toward the driver's side, Vivian glanced back at him. She was only slightly surprised to see Thane perched in the center of the back seat, leaning forward.

"Movie time! Buttered popcorn, jujubes and a tall soda."

"Not tonight, little brother. Out. We can chat when I get home."

"Alright, alright. But if he reaches into the popcorn tub exactly when you do and then pretends like it was an accident, he's totally trying to be smooth!"

"Go!" Vivian laughed, as Grant opened the door and slid behind the wheel.

"Ready?"

"Ready." Vivian waved at her dad and Rebecca, who still

stood in the frame of the opened door, their arms wrapped around one another as they shivered in the chilled air which had given in to the coolness of night. A cloudless sky hung above, blanketed with twinkling dots of starlight.

Grant drove smoothly down the narrow road. The weeping willows' leaves had been replaced with a layer of shiny, white snow that sparkled in the moonlight. Rather than looking sad and hunched over, their branches looked strong and beautiful. Their thick trunks could withstand the gusts of wind that slammed against them in the winter storms, which had deposited the snow hugging the sides of the road in large heaps. Vivian watched them blur past.

Slipping the loose braid behind her shoulder, she gazed at her reflection in the blackened window. She brushed away the loose hair that hung strategically across her forehead. Though her scars reflected back at her, she smiled at her reflection.

Grant reached for her hand and flashed his perfect, full-dimpled grin. "You look amazing."

"Thanks." She smiled back. She felt amazing.

ABOUT THE AUTHOR

JESSICA FREEBURG has always been inquisitive and loves the challenges of all that life, and the afterlife, has to offer. Her fascination with the strange and fantastic fuels many of her creative works. She embraces the fringe and relishes in the examination of what others may take for granted. As the founder of Ghost Stories, Inc., Jessica has performed paranormal investigations at a variety of reportedly haunted locations. She has contributed to the popular paranormal program Darkness Radio and serves on the editorial staff of FATE Magazine. She lives in Lakeville, MN with her husband and three children.

GREAT STORIES. NO GUILT.

www.cleanreads.com

CPSIA information can be obtained at www.ICGtesting.com
Printed in the USA
LVOW07s2158270116

472595LV00002B/142/P